A NOVEL BASED ON THE LIFE OF
COSIMO DE' MEDICI

FIRST
AMONG EQUALS

Francesco Massaccesi

W0010483

THE
MENTORIS
PROJECT

Barbera Foundation, Inc.
P.O. Box 1019
Temple City, CA 91780

Copyright © 2018 Barbera Foundation, Inc.
Cover photo: Azoor Photo / Alamy Stock Photo
Cover design: Suzanne Turpin

More information at www.mentorisproject.org

ISBN: 978-1-947431-18-8

Library of Congress Control Number: 2018957763

The Mentoris Project is a series of novels and biographies about the lives of great Italians and Italian-Americans: men and women who have changed history through their contributions as scientists, inventors, explorers, thinkers, and creators. The Barbera Foundation sponsors this series in the hope that, like a mentor, each book will inspire the reader to discover how she or he can make a positive contribution to society.

Contents

Foreword

First and foremost, Mentor was a person. We tend to think of the word *mentor* as a noun (a mentor) or a verb (to mentor), but there is a very human dimension embedded in the term. Mentor appears in Homer's *Odyssey* as the old friend entrusted to care for Odysseus's household and his son Telemachus during the Trojan War. When years pass and Telemachus sets out to search for his missing father, the goddess Athena assumes the form of Mentor to accompany him. The human being welcomes a human form for counsel. From its very origins, becoming a mentor is a transcendent act; it carries with it something of the holy.

The Barbera Foundation's Mentoris Project sets out on an Athena-like mission: We hope the books that form this series will be an inspiration to all those who are seekers, to those of the twenty-first century who are on their own odysseys, trying to find enduring principles that will guide them to a spiritual home. The stories that comprise the series are all deeply human. These books dramatize the lives of great Italians and Italian-Americans whose stories bridge the ancient and the modern, taking many forms, just as Athena did, but always holding up a light for those living today.

Whether in novel form or traditional biography, these

books plumb the individual characters of our heroes' journeys. The power of storytelling has always been to envelop the reader in a vivid and continuous dream, and to forge a link with the subject. Our goal is for that link to guide the reader home with a new inspiration.

What is a mentor? A guide, a moral compass, an inspiration. A friend who points you toward true north. We hope that the Mentoris Project will become that friend, and it will help us all transcend our daily lives with something that can only be called holy.

—Robert J. Barbera, President, Barbera Foundation
—Ken LaZebnik, Editor, The Mentoris Project

Chapter One

LEGENDS AND LEGACIES

The Mugello valley had never been so beautiful.

Catching his reflection in the freezing cold waters of the stream where he had stopped to wash his face, Charlemagne paused and then looked up to take in the landscape around him—this place in the Tuscan countryside seemed suspended in a state of enchanted beauty.

The blissful nature of the Mugello contradicted its very name, for that tangible angle of Eden had been named after its first conquerors, the fierce and aggressive tribe of the Magelli, who, after moving from their original area in the Liguria region, had landed in Tuscany after many peregrinations and battles.

But Charlemagne ignored this.

What did matter to him during those fleeting moments so far removed from his courtly life, his duties, and his power was to be free to ride his horse along the interminable woods and the banks of the Sieve River, to admire fully the riches of that fertile land.

Like many before him, Charlemagne had discovered that the wide Mugello valley was the ideal place to hunt. It was a reserve fit for princes, noblemen, and even emperors with a bored but impetuous disposition.

While being a guest of the noble Ubaldini family, who had command over the Mugello fief, Charlemagne prepared himself to hunt deer accompanied by a handful of loyal men chosen amongst the inhabitants of the area.

However, early on that fateful day, the Emperor Charlemagne had unexpectedly fallen ill; it was a sudden ailment that some judged to be pneumonia, while others thought it could be rheumatic fever or an infection.

Whatever the cause of illness, Charlemagne was dying in one of the most beautiful places he had ever set his eyes upon.

Only one man, a local *mugellano* of a charitable nature and versed in the medical arts, had understood that it was crucial to intervene without further ado. He saw Charlemagne not simply as a great man who had been made emperor by the grace of God, but also as a human being who was fighting fiercely for his life.

That man carried with him a set of small metal cups for practicing the medical art of bloodletting, an ancient technique used by doctors and surgeons for more than two thousand years to remove the "bad" blood from the patient's body.

The metal cups, similar to small balls, were applied on the emperor's body; he quickly recovered from his illness, almost as if touched by divine intervention.

Full of gratitude, Charlemagne conceded to that skilled and generous man the highest possible honor—he gave him and his family a name and a coat of arms inspired by his medical knowledge that would resonate for centuries to come.

~

"That man of medicine was our ancestor. Even though we don't know much about him, thanks to his charitable soul our family is proud to bear the name Medici. Even today, we bear the red cups on our emblem to remember him and the future he created for our whole family."

"Is this true, Grandfather?"

"Every story, as fictitious as it may sound or even be, has something that we can take and make some good from. It's your choice what you're going to take from what I've just told you. It's up to you to be wise."

The time is a Florentine summer in the year 1460. The place is the Medici home on the Via Larga, a building so modern and perfectly structured that all Tuscan palaces of a certain importance built at the time used it as their model.

The aging Cosimo de' Medici, banker, patron of the arts, intellectual, and de facto ruler of Florence, the first among equals, was spending his afternoon there in the company of his grandson Lorenzo.

The young boy was a child, yet in a few years he would gain the nickname of Magnificent and be known as one of the main personalities of the Italian Renaissance.

The story Cosimo narrated was probably just a legend. Each story is born of something, be it myth or reality, and the truth about the origins of the Medici family was—and still is—a mystery, lost in the fog of time.

The tale of the metal cups was considered by some a derogatory joke spread about by the French court, and it was, in any case, only one of many hypotheses and legends connected with the family's name and shield.

"You see, Lorenzo, the origins of our family aren't as ancient as those of Florence, but they're equally, if not more, mysterious."

Cosimo could have never guessed that the true origin of the Medici family name and shield would remain a point of contention among later historians, who, just like the scholars who preceded them over the centuries, would ponder over it with the most disparate theories.

According to the supporters of the "medical theory," one piece of evidence was the choice of the two patron saints of the family, Cosmas and Damian, medics and thaumaturges who helped the poor and the needy. Other historians regarded the choice of the two patron saints as dictated exclusively by the similarity between their profession and the family's surname, and by the assonance between the Cosimo and Cosmas names.

For some, the balls represented bitter oranges that the Medici traded with the Orient and a large part of Italy. Others saw in them the symbol of the weights merchants employed to measure goods and coins. And yet others believed they were an alternative representation of the shield of the corporation of which the family was part.

Some historians have attributed to the Medici shield a heroic origin. One of the earliest members of the family, Averardo de' Medici, was an officer in Charlemagne's army and had become a hero in the Mugello area after defeating a giant, also named Mugello, who was swaggering about the region. The distinctive figures on the Medici coat of arms would have been inspired by the blows left by the giant's iron mace on the knight's shield.

Young Lorenzo considered the account he had just heard. The story of the healer was not entirely convincing to him and he still had a few questions to ask.

"But, Grandfather Cosimo, why are the cups on our emblem

red?" The question, springing from the lively and curious mind of Lorenzo, triggered an almost imperceptible smile on Cosimo's face.

"You see, my grandson, when you're sick, you can take a white, red, or golden pill. A white pill is mostly made of sugar, and its effects often bland and innocuous. A golden pill may very well be effective, but can sometimes create great turmoil all over the body, and only the richest people from the elite can afford them. A red pill, on the other hand, is more common; most people can afford it and its effects cure the body without putting it in turmoil."

"What does that mean, Grandfather?"

"That while other families might use a golden symbol on their emblems to represent their status above others, we Medici chose red because we feel closer to our fellow citizens. Do you understand now?"

The young boy nodded gently, lowering his eyes. "And this other story is true?"

Another imperceptible smile. "Remember my words about stories, Lorenzo."

Lorenzo raised his eyes again. "Tell me another one, please, Grandfather."

The boy's imploring eyes were fixed on the aging patriarch. The two of them were having such a lovely day together.

Lorenzo's long and narrow nose, already pointy in his pre-adolescent features, seemed to tremble with the anticipation and excitement of Cosimo's answer. Impatiently, he kept throwing glances toward the door of the patriarch's study left ajar. The muffled noises and voices coming from the servants as they did their chores and from the rest of his family going about their day seemed to disturb him.

Cosimo's pale, lanky hand lifted gently a finely decorated porcelain cup filled with one of those infusions of medicinal herbs to be drunk in the morning. They were all utterly disgusting but Cosimo, always methodical, had accepted those supposedly therapeutic mixtures and many other obligations from his many doctors (who certainly weren't descendants of his legendary ancestor) as part of his daily routine. As soon as he emptied the cup, Lorenzo was already refilling it with more infusion.

"Here, Grandfather. It will make you feel good," said the boy.

That small gesture meant so much for young Lorenzo. He was extremely fond of his grandfather and wanted him to be healthy and well forever.

Clean-shaven and with his hair covered by a cap made of light fabric, Cosimo appeared well groomed and, just like Lorenzo, dressed in a fashionable but not ostentatious manner.

Sitting on an old wooden chair—perhaps even older than he was—Cosimo was holding in his lap an ancient-looking volume in Latin. In that room, one of his many study rooms, Cosimo and Lorenzo were surrounded by all sorts of books—new and old, slender and bulky—and an array of other marvels that would have astonished old and modern and intellectuals alike.

Cosimo's physical aspect betrayed his advanced age—his face was a tapestry of lines and signs that pulsated gently with the steady, slow rhythm of his breath. His heart could not be tired out and his body bore the marks of arthritis and gout, an illness that afflicted his family like a curse. It had been one of the causes in the death of his beloved brother Lorenzo, twenty years before.

Cosimo tried to clear his throat—speaking too much and

for too long, even to his adored grandson, was not an effort to be taken on lightly.

Of course, he did not lack stories to tell. Throughout his life he had listened and learned, and it was thanks to this, in combination with his skills for business and a capacity to speak and act in the right way at the right time, that Cosimo had achieved his success and position.

His voice, once so bright and clear but also capable of being so thunderous that his enemies and peers were left trembling and subdued, was now nothing more than a whisper, a soft breath from a life that had seen and achieved all that was within man's reach.

Cosimo touched his lips lightly. They were parched and chafed, like those of a pilgrim stranded in the desert, he thought. That was an intriguing parallel, something so far and detached from his daily life that Cosimo would have found it bizarre and almost funny in another day and age.

It was not the right time to let his mind drift away, but Cosimo found himself momentarily lost in the memory of that short time in his life when he had been forced by his enemies to stay away from his own town. But, no. It was not the time then to dwell on that memory.

Cosimo drank the second cup of herbal tea, trying to forget its foul taste.

His body might have been showing signs of physical decline, but his mind was eager and lucid as ever, forced to observe the gradual failure of his body now marred by the ravages of time and of a life that had already been much longer than the standards of the period. The warmth and pungent taste of the tea hit Cosimo straight in his senses and he finally felt reinvigorated enough to answer Lorenzo's question.

"Do you have any special requests, my grandson?"

The child lowered his head, seemingly embarrassed to give such an unoriginal answer. They both knew very well which ones their favorite stories were.

The old patriarch was amused at his grandson's reaction, and behind Cosimo's expression there was a mind reflecting upon life and death, the past and the future.

As pragmatic as he had ever been, Cosimo was perfectly aware that he was living the last years of his life. The long conversations with Lorenzo and his grandson's company, however, managed to make the weight of his inevitable fate somewhat more bearable. He would have been ready, though, to renounce all his riches just to have the chance to live longer and see his grandchildren—especially Lorenzo—grow into adulthood.

Cosimo loved all of his grandchildren, but there was something special about Lorenzo, something that seemed to bring their individual destinies together in an unprecedented manner.

It was perhaps because Cosimo found in Lorenzo the acceptance of his own mortality, a way to understand that the link between their lives indicated that his long life and all his achievements really had meaning after all and would never be dispelled. But it was more than that—Cosimo did see in Lorenzo and his brother Giuliano that period of his youth he had spent in the company of his own brother.

"Very well, Lorenzo, our next story will be . . ." The room's door opened with an annoyingly creaking sound that interrupted Cosimo in mid-sentence.

Piero, the first son of Cosimo—Lorenzo's father—appeared on the threshold. His sickly look and his face so prematurely wizened had gained him the nickname of *il Gottoso*, "the Gouty." Gout did indeed afflict him, together with an array of other

fevers that forced him to spend long periods of time in bed or traveling around Tuscany in search of curative waters and other remedies.

On that particular day, as if by a miracle, Piero was standing straight and solid on the threshold of his father's study room. With a low and respectful tone of voice, he said, "Father, I have just returned and I wanted to . . ."

Cosimo stopped with a simple gesture, asking him to hold off long enough to give him time to take leave from his grandson. Piero had just returned from one of his therapeutic journeys and wanted to greet his father. Lorenzo was looking at Cosimo with a disappointed face.

"What now, Grandfather?"

"Now I reckon I owe you a story, son. Go to your father. He's worthy of your attention more than I am."

Lorenzo ran to his father, who greeted him with a soft caress on his head and a proud father's face.

"Don't tire your grandfather too much. Go join your brother Giuliano, Lorenzo. Your tutor, Gentile, is ready to begin today's lesson."

Lorenzo seemed to hesitate for an instant but Cosimo reassured him.

"Go learn, my child, cultivate your mind. I will still be here when you finish."

Lorenzo ran off, ready for his lesson. Piero's words referred to Gentile de' Becchi, a native of Urbino whose fame as a scholar and an intellectual had attracted Cosimo's attention. He had become the tutor of Piero's sons, teaching them Latin and Italian poetry and prose. Gentile would always remain loyal to the Medici family and later took various roles during Lorenzo's government.

Giuliano, who later died during the Pazzi Conspiracy against the Medici family in 1478, was not Lorenzo's only sibling. Apart from Piero's illegitimate son Giovanni, Lorenzo and Giuliano had three sisters: Bianca, Maria, and Lucrezia, who was known as Nannina, like Cosimo's own mother. Just like their brothers, the three girls had been educated following the precepts and the highest standards of humanist culture.

What was humanism? As a way to soothe the cultural decline of the Middle Ages and generate an artistic and intellectual rebirth, Italian men of letters started a movement that sought a return to the ideals of classical antiquity. This movement became one of the greatest achievements of the Renaissance. After the Middle Ages, which were characterized by an ascetic vision of humanity, humanism placed man at the center of everything and regarded him as capable of dominating all life and shaping his own destiny thanks to his intelligence and free will.

This new philosophy did not refute the principles and original purity of the Christian belief, which according to intellectuals had been lost in the previous centuries. Rather, it allowed humanity to experience a sentiment of guilt-free hedonism and naturalism— feelings that permitted man to search for pleasure and enjoy nature in and of itself. Humanists were well versed in rhetoric, moral philosophy, poetry, grammar, and ancient history; even the name derived from Greco-Roman roots, based on the concept of famed Roman orator and intellectual Cicero of *humanitas*, an ideal series of positive tracts every human being should possess to fulfill his public service and live a decent private life. Cicero's definition of humanitas—similarly formulated by Romans such as Terence and Pliny the Younger—went along with the classic Greek views of *philanthropia*, "the love for mankind," and *paideia*, the physical and mental education of the youth.

Cosimo looked Piero in the eyes. His son seemed to feel better than usual, even though his complexion suggested that he was prey of one of his usual fevers.

"I'm still not easily tired, my son," said Cosimo.

"You're still the sharpest mind in all of Tuscany, Father."

"How are your precious daughters?" asked Cosimo. "I hope they're having their lessons right now too."

"They are well and they miss their grandparents, Father. And, to answer your question, I believe they're busy with Latin," answered Piero.

"Very good. I'd love to have a chat with their tutor to see how they're doing. What about you, then? Would I be mistaken to say you're just back from the Petriolo curative baths?"

"No, Father, I'd have risked running my fever too high."

"Where's your brother Giovanni? I haven't seen him all day."

Piero hesitated, seemingly looking for a convincing reply. "He's . . . he's indisposed today." Cosimo understood perfectly well the reason behind that hesitation and he already knew the truthful answer to his question.

"Did he drink too much this time, or has he returned too late?" Cosimo reached his own conclusions even before Piero could reply. "I see. Too many celebrations and too much wine."

"Only the latter, I'm afraid."

Even though Cosimo loved his sons, neither Piero nor Giovanni had ever managed to meet the hopes and expectations he had for them.

Cosimo had always hoped that his sons would continue his political and financial activities and, as was the custom for all aristocratic families at the time, Piero and Giovanni had also been educated by the best tutors available.

The two had very different personalities: Piero was introverted and held back by his numerous ailments, while Giovanni was bright but uneven, both in his studies and in keeping up with his duties.

Where Piero was austere and serious, Giovanni was lighthearted and prone to over-enjoy life's pleasures. He loved parties and staying out all night (and for a period, he had even managed to drag Piero with him). Giovanni was also a more complex personality, yet with a profound soul.

Memories of his sons' complicated study records appeared in Cosimo's mind. He remembered how he had questioned their tutor, the great humanist Poggio Bracciolini, about his sons' progress.

"Does Piero apply himself?" At Cosimo's inquiry about Piero's philosophy lessons, Bracciolini had looked resigned and beaten.

"Piero has ambitions too high to be reached but only manages to grasp concepts that are closer to him."

"What about Giovanni?" asked Cosimo, who'd known Bracciolini for a long time and considered him a personal friend he could always trust.

"Giovanni? Well, his mind is certainly bright but he's in dire need to concentrate on his grammar exercises if he wants to retain anything he's learned so far!"

Despite their personal limitations, flaws, and vices, Cosimo's sons grew to love and protect art and culture, thus becoming sponsors of many artists.

Cosimo introduced them, from a very young age, to the

world of business and put them at work as apprentices in his banks. Although he had clearly understood that neither of his sons had inherited his financial acumen, he never gave up on involving them directly in the family's affairs.

Their business sense proved to be inconsequential, but they did gain some success in their political activities. Both sons traveled as ambassadors and took political offices in Florence.

Just like Piero and Cosimo, even Giovanni had resigned himself—mainly for the love for his family—to follow the directions of a wide group of doctors.

"Is Giovanni following the doctors' orders, Piero?"

Piero started to list the latest orders the doctors had imposed on Giovanni. "To live in a salubrious place. To eat well. To avoid drinking too much. To avoid sleeping in the afternoon. To avoid excesses of all kinds . . ."

"And to take pills, syrups, all kinds of medicinal poultices. Every day, more than once a day," Cosimo went on.

Father and son looked at each other with complicity.

"I now see Giovanni's binge last night in a better light. I would have allowed myself to be driven by my vices after hearing just half of that list," said Cosimo.

"Not even an army of doctors could force Giovanni to follow their rules. Even if they're for his own good."

Cosimo repeated those words with a trace of bitterness in his voice. "For his own good, yes."

Piero took a little book out of his pocket. Cosimo regarded it with curiosity.

"What is that?" he asked.

"A new collection of poems," said Piero. "It's for you." Cosimo took the volume in his hands and regarded it attentively.

"Thank you, Piero. A new addition to my libraries."

"It's from Lucrezia, Father. She obtained it for you in Siena."

"Lucrezia is the finest mind in the family. And often its only real man," Cosimo said with a voice full of the admiration he felt for his daughter-in-law.

Piero nodded approvingly. His wife took care of the family and of Piero's own well-being, even of his business, when Piero was too unwell to do that himself. For this reason, he did not feel undermined or offended by his father's words.

According to the custom of great families of the time, Cosimo had made every effort to find wives for his two sons, hoping to instill new life into Piero and calm down Giovanni's fiery spirits this way.

For Piero, Cosimo chose Lucrezia Tornabuoni, daughter of the merchant Francesco Tornabuoni, an ally and supporter of Cosimo even during his most difficult moments.

Lucrezia was the right choice for Piero, not just because they shared a mutual love for culture and patronage, but also from the point of view of alliances, because the Tornabuoni were supporters of the Medici and also one of the most prominent Florentine families.

Cosimo's esteem for her was certainly not unfounded.

Lucrezia was an extremely cultivated woman; friends with contemporary intellectuals, a poetess, and a woman of letters; a benefactor of the poor, a backer of craftsmen and entrepreneurs. She was also a shrewd businesswoman, and continued to be one of the family's keystones even after Cosimo's death, as Piero eventually became bedridden with gout.

"What is good for Florence and Tuscany is also good for the Medici family," Lucrezia would say when someone asked about her businesses and charitable work.

Finding a wife for Giovanni was more difficult for Cosimo, as Giovanni was not inclined toward being "trapped" in a marriage.

Now Cosimo's mind returned to the memory of a letter that a friend addressed to Giovanni. "Do not move from where you are and don't come back to Florence, otherwise your father will force you to take a wife! You'll end up stinking of rotten sulfur like your brother!"

In spite of the complaints, Giovanni married Ginevra Alessandri, who came from a family originally part of the Albizzi, among the most ferocious rivals to the Medici.

If the wedding of Piero with Lucrezia was mainly aimed toward reinforcing the *Banco* and financial interests, the one between Giovanni and Ginevra was aimed toward a political and domestic reconciliation between Cosimo and the descendants of his determined adversaries.

Cosimo also had a third son, Carlo, born out of a relationship with a Circassian slave named Maddalena, who had been bought in Venice and kept at home as a servant, the custom of rich Italians at that time.

The importation of slaves into Florence was a consequence of frequent plague epidemics, which had decimated part of the city's manpower during the fourteenth century. The most requested slaves were young women to keep at home as servants, often becoming concubines of the master of the house. As per the custom during that period, the birth of an illegitimate child would not bring dishonor to a family, nor did it perturb its balances. The child would be raised with his or her legitimate siblings.

Carlo was healthier and more sensible than his brothers, and had followed the ecclesiastical path, earning esteem and praise from both his father and the religious authorities, especially for his appointment to the Prato Cathedral.

Besides, having Medici blood in his veins, Carlo also knew exactly what to do when it came to financial matters. And, to that acumen, in spite of his religious vocation and quiet personality, he connected memories that could still put a smile on Cosimo's face.

"The water that runs in the fountain here in your villa is so pure and clear, Father," Carlo said once when visiting Cosimo in one of his country houses. "So pure that it could go through my hands as if they were transparent."

Before Cosimo could answer, Lorenzo, who was even younger then, put himself between his grandfather and uncle and, without thinking twice, exclaimed, "But if that water were made of money—you would never let it go through your hands, Uncle!"

Struck by family ailments but not inclined to abandon his lifestyle, Giovanni would die in 1463, an event that put Cosimo in a state of dejection. Cosimo himself followed his second-born son to the grave shortly after. With the death of Giovanni and Cosimo, Piero was then left with Florence's destiny in his hands. He was forced to manage difficult situations up until his death, and the handover to Lorenzo.

But in this moment, in the year 1460, seventy-five-year-old Cosimo was pensive about the future of his family.

"We must be patient with your brother, Piero. Not unlike you, he has . . ."

Before Cosimo could finish, the sound of laughter and quick steps in the hallway made the two men turn their heads.

Lorenzo was running with a pitcher full of water in his hand, laughing as he tried to carry it without spilling a single drop.

"Father! Grandfather! Look how strong I am!"

Piero addressed him severely. "Lorenzo, what did I tell you?"

"But *maestro* Gentile wanted some water!"

"If I see that you spilled even one drop on your grandfather's floor, I'll . . ." threatened Piero.

Lorenzo ran away before his father had time to finish. Cosimo and Piero looked at each other.

"At least his siblings are less of a handful," sighed Piero.

Cosimo continued. "You're two intelligent men. Despite his lows, your brother has already done much with his life—as you have—despite all your maladies."

"I know, Father. I know Giovanni's vices haven't completely enslaved him. That was a risk when he was younger, but now I see the man he has become," replied Piero. "It's just that ever since his son Cosimino succumbed to his illness last year, I fear Giovanni is pretending to be happy despite feeling hollow inside."

Cosimo closed his fists; a deep sadness came upon him. His son Giovanni had tried to have children twice more, but they died shortly after birth.

"Seeing the happiness of your children must be punishment for him . . . Cosimino, named after me, didn't even live to be ten years old. And here I am, an old man, something from the past, a relic."

Piero tried to console his father, but struggled to find the right words.

"Father, you . . ." Noticing his father's lost gaze, Piero stopped. "Is something troubling you?"

"Do you ever think of the future, Piero?"

"If this is about our family future, I understand your concerns, but . . ." Cosimo stopped him. One thing he didn't want was to be pitied or misunderstood.

"No. That's not what I'm talking about," said the old man. "The family will resist as it always has. And Florence will stand with it."

Piero wasn't understanding. "Then, what is it?"

Cosimo became even more cryptic. "Do you ever think of the future *and* the past?"

Cosimo moved toward a pile of books on a shelf—ancient volumes, dusty and precious, full of history and wisdom. It was just a tiny fraction of the legacy Cosimo would leave to the world, yet so inestimable. Cosimo started to caress the books' spines, lost in his thoughts. Piero understood that it might be best to leave him on his own.

"I will see you later, Father."

Sitting on a chair and surrounded by a dozen books taken down from the shelves, Cosimo continued to reflect. His mind was still full of doubts.

"*How has my life been? Where did all the years go?*" Cosimo asked himself.

Shortly after, a feminine hand gently opened the door. It was Contessina de' Bardi, wife of Cosimo for more than thirty years.

Contessina hadn't been named as such because of a title of nobility. She was given the name in honor of the famous countess Matilda of Canossa, a historical figure in Florence's destiny toward the end of the year 1000, through her role as a faithful ally of the pope in the struggle against Emperor Henry IV, and a proponent of the autonomy of Florentines.

Contessina was the same age as Cosimo, and they were each

from a prominent Florence family—their marriage was politically important. The Bardi, once among the first European bankers, had lost most of their riches and importance following a missed reimbursement of money lent to the King of England, Edward III, but they had subsequently managed to get back their wealth thanks to cautious investments and land ownership.

Pragmatic and calm, Contessina did not have the brilliance nor the intellectual passions of a woman like Lucrezia, and spent her days dealing with house chores and family matters and taking care of relationships with the merchants who supplied the family properties with food and other goods. She found happiness in caring for the domestic environment and her love for her husband, children, and the rest of the family.

The relationship with her husband had never dimmed, even with Cosimo's exile while Contessina lived out of the city, always managing part of the family's affairs, nor with the birth of the illegitimate son.

"Since you left, I haven't received any more news of you, and this week seemed like a year," wrote Contessina to her husband. "Take care in eating well or that health problem of yours will start again," she wrote to one of her sons. Those letters—out of which around thirty survived—written to Cosimo or to her sons when they were far away, were full of love and concern, and demonstrated Contessina's calm and reflexive nature, as well as her practical sense. She was a woman who never lost heart in the face of a challenge but instead immediately looked for a solution.

"Piero is worried about you," said Contessina now to her husband.

"Piero is always worried about me. And so is Giovanni," replied Cosimo.

"He told me something's troubling you. Perhaps . . ."

"Perhaps what?"

"He, and maybe even Giovanni, think you're not proud of them."

"I'm proud and full of love when I see all of you. And despite what they might think, my love includes both Piero and Giovanni."

Cosimo was inscrutable. Not even Contessina seemed to understand what was ailing him.

"You're thoughtful, even more than usual. It's true, then. Something is troubling you."

Something's troubling you. Cosimo kept hearing this phrase in his head. Then he answered his wife.

"I've spent all my life thinking. About business, about Florence, about *thinkers*, about my loved ones. But now I'm constantly thinking about myself, about the meaning of my life."

Contessina tried to move the conversation in another direction, hoping to awaken his love and sense of pride for his grandchildren, and thus lift up his mood.

"I saw Lorenzo and the other little ones scurrying by . . ." she mentioned.

"Fate has been kind to us. Piero has been blessed with wonderful children and we have been blessed with wonderful grandchildren. Giuliano, Nannina, and Bianca will do much with their lives, but Lorenzo . . . Lorenzo is the one who will take this family forward into the future."

"Lorenzo and Giuliano always remind me of you and your brother."

Cosimo wasn't expecting that reply, and for a moment he remained stunned, lost between happiness and pride.

"It's the best sentiment anyone could have ever said to me."

"I might say that love is blinding you, blinding *us*, but . . ."

"... You can't."

"Yes, Cosimo, I can't. We've been blessed."

"When I look Lorenzo in the eyes, I see ..."

"The future."

Cosimo opened a closet, taking out a stack of papers bearing his writing. Only one look was enough for Contessina to understand what they were.

"Your ... ?"

"You have to tell your story before you start forgetting it." Cosimo took the stack of papers and locked them in the drawer.

"Maybe Lorenzo will hear my story from me, in person, and not just from my memories."

"Your legacy will last forever, no matter what."

Forever ... forever ... The words echoed in Cosimo's mind. Thoughts were vanquished by memories, which would increasingly come to the surface to replace the present.

Chapter Two

TEACHINGS

"Keep your head down and focus on your exercises, Cosimo."

In the Camaldolese abbey of *Santa Maria degli Angeli*, Saint Mary of the Angels, Roberto de' Rossi was carrying out his role as tutor of two very young boys, Cosimo and Lorenzo.

"Yes, Teacher," Cosimo replied without lifting his head from the exercises. His seriousness and dedication in his studies already provided hints as to the man he would become.

It was the year 1400; Cosimo was just eleven. The fourteenth century had just ended, closing a difficult, complex period for Florence.

At the beginning of the 1300s, the city had reached its zenith in economy, culture, and arts, but the following years had brought internal and external struggles: social and financial crises, a period of semi-tyranny, and the great plague epidemic of 1348, which swept through Europe to reduce the urban population to less than half, just as during the dark times of the barbaric invasions of previous centuries.

In spite of all this, Florence survived, too proud to fall without getting back up.

"Fruit! Fresh fruit! Get the best fruit here!"

This determination could be seen in the shouting of peddlers, who arrived from the countryside on foot with their baskets, after having left several hours before, and who would roam the streets of Florence to earn what they needed for the day. Men, women, old people, and children, so far removed from Cosimo and Lorenzo's world that the two young brothers sometimes observed the peddlers from the height of the room where the lessons took place.

Their tutor, de' Rossi, wasn't paying attention to the peddlers, but he would linger to look at laborers and merchants carrying goods and materials as they headed toward their own shops and laboratories. *How many of them*, he asked himself silently, *were aware of their importance for the prosperity of Florence?*

The city leaders kept the financial organization of Florence stabilized; this was one of the few consistent values throughout the decades of uncertainty that had just passed. As had indeed been happening for more than one hundred years, merchants, craftsmen, and representatives of the various professional activities organized themselves into corporate associations, the so-called *arti*, to regulate the labor and growth of the city.

These corporations were born around 1182, when some merchants had founded the *Arte dei Mercatanti*, or *Arte di Calimala*, dedicated to handwoven fabrics; the economic development had been such that in a short period of time associations for the most varied categories of merchants and artisans had visibly multiplied.

Subdivided in *arti maggiori* (major corporations) and *arti minori* (minor corporations), the first were endowed with far greater influence and power compared to the latter. This contrast between corporations affected the social landscape by dividing part of the population into those who were called *popolo grasso* and *popolo minuto*, namely fat people and small people.

The failure of the *Tumulto dei Ciompi* in 1378, a revolt of minor wool laborers (lowly laborers and errand boys of all trades were called *ciompi*, and they were considered to be the lowest strata of society) yearning to improve their economic and political position, contributed to a shift in the city's rules from a democratic one to an oligarchic one, supported by the rich mercantile bourgeoisie. The appointments remained unchanged, with the *gonfaloniere*, the *priori*, and the various *consigli*, but in reality the city's politics were in the hands of three people: Maso degli Albizzi, Niccolò da Uzzano, and Gino Capponi, all counseled and supported by a big number of allies.

Hence Cosimo and Lorenzo were living their formative years in a city shaken by social change, successes, failures, and continuous developments.

Lorenzo was looking out of the tiny window from inside the small room used for the lessons. Almost all the Florentine great families' favorites studied in the monastery, including the Albizzi.

"The sun is shining! Can we go outside and play, Teacher?"

"Only if you listen carefully and finish your exercises too, Lorenzo. Learn from your brother."

Cosimo, the older of the two brothers, was born in 1389, six years before Lorenzo. He was considered the more intellectually gifted of the two.

Cosimo and Lorenzo weren't only children: Damiano and Antonio, born in 1390 and 1398, died very young, while the sole daughter, about whom so little information has reached us to the point of doubting her very existence, died of an illness shortly before her marriage.

De' Rossi, together with other intellectuals, had been chosen especially by Giovanni di Bicci, the father of the two boys, with the intention to give his own children the best possible culture. Hiring de' Rossi had been a particularly shrewd choice, as he was known for his thorough knowledge of Greek and Latin.

Moreover, de' Rossi had been one of the first Florentine humanists, a follower of the Byzantine scholar Emanuele Crisolora and of Coluccio Salutati, an intellectual and political figure who was crucial in the development of humanism in Florence.

"*Homo faber fortunae suae*," de' Rossi often repeated to his pupils. "Every man is the maker of his own fortune. Remember that when you do your exercises or feel too tired to keep on studying," he told them.

"Yes, Teacher," Cosimo and Lorenzo answered simultaneously.

De' Rossi had been part of the first wave of Florentine humanism that had gained popularity between the 1300s and 1400s, when chancelleries that maintained relationships with foreign states—by writing letters to princes and governments and supervising the truthfulness of official documents and historical events—had slowly become places of cultural formation and discussion.

And thus the Republican government had started attributing crucial roles to the best humanists, who would then become civic humanists, intellectuals capable of handling public and political offices. Humanism was very much part of the intellectual formation of Cosimo, who would follow those ideals throughout his life.

But those years were still far away. During those days at the monastery, an equivalent of a prestigious boarding school, Cosimo developed a love for culture, becoming well versed in Latin and Greek, and even managing to acquire a good knowledge of Arabic. When Lorenzo was busy with other lessons, Cosimo and de' Rossi would often take walks along the monastery's cloisters.

"How much do you know about Florence, Cosimo?" asked de' Rossi.

Cosimo didn't reply, unsure of what to say.

"To not know what came before us is like staying children forever," continued de' Rossi.

"Cicero said so," readily answered Cosimo, understanding the master's Latin quote. Teacher and master stopped in front of an old tree, whose rugged bark made it look centuries old. Cosimo lightly touched that coarse surface, feeling small in front of nature's magnificence.

"How old do you think this tree is, Cosimo? Younger or older than Florence?"

"Older . . . maybe?"

De' Rossi laughed heartily, confronted with the little ingenuity of one of the pupils he was most proud of.

"In a different time, people would have replied that only Flora could answer that."

Flora was the Roman goddess of flowers and springtime. De' Rossi's unending love and knowledge of Greek and Latin culture obviously included the origins of Florence.

"Just like humanity itself, Cosimo, Florence goes far back in time. Remember, if you want to understand the present and plan the future, you need to know the past."

Florence's past has always been up for debate and examination. Just like the Medici family name, the true etymological root of the name Florence has still not yet been entirely ascertained. Some studies date it back to the early Etruscan settlements, while others connect it to the Roman times, when the place's name was *Florentia*.

Some historians link the name to the Etruscan king Florinus or to a Roman general by the same name. Others explain the name from the fact that the city passed under Roman rule during the period of the *Floralia*, celebrations in honor of the goddess Flora.

Finally, other theories claim that the Italian name of the city—Firenze—could be connected to the Etruscan word *Birenz*, or "land between the rivers," and thus a direct reference to its proximity of the Arno and its tributary streams.

"It was really very different from what it is today, you see," said de' Rossi to his student. "The first Romans who founded their colony here were veterans, and Florence was the fortified village where they would have spent their older years. Caesar or Lucius Cornelius Sulla led to its founding, or maybe Emperor Augustus."

"Will we ever know for sure?" asked Cosimo.

"No, we won't. Time does its best to erase as much as it can. But don't be disappointed, because even when we know the past, we cannot know everything. And not knowing everything, that is one of the prices we must pay as mortal men." Pupil and mentor had resumed their walk, as the fragrance of seasonal fruit, fresh vegetables, and cooked food sold by the peddlers spread through the air, flooding the cloister with aromas and sensations.

Cosimo admired the architectural structure of the monastery, whose foundations had been modified and expanded toward the end of the thirteenth century, due to the efforts of Guittone d'Arezzo, a well-known religious poet.

The area was rural, located outside of the city walls, but the city had already taken a liking to the Camaldolese monks, as they actively participated in public life.

"And tell me, Cosimo, why and how Roman Florence became a powerful city?"

This time Cosimo replied without any hesitation. "The proximity of the Via Cassia, the navigability of the Arno River, the fertility of our countryside, the net of communications and commercial exchanges both on land and sea."

"Correct. And what protected it?"

"The wall perimeter. The city was built according to the traditional Roman structure of the *castrum*, with straight streets crossing at perpendicular angles, and two main streets—the *decumanus maximus* and *cardo maximus*—converging on a central square and leading to the settlement's four doors."

"And what was the name of the square?"

"The *forum urbis*."

"Very good, Cosimo. You're a student who never disappoints a teacher."

"But I am still a child, Teacher. I still have much to learn."

"Indeed, but you won't be a child forever, nor will your thirst for knowledge ever be satiated."

"Is it good to remember such a distant past if we no longer have any connection to it?"

De' Rossi stopped. He wanted Cosimo to remember what he was about to say. "It doesn't matter that we haven't lived at the time of Caesar, Augustus, or Dante. When we remember them and what they've done, their legacy lives. And we must act as such. But remember that we should not employ all of our time in contemplation. We must be actively involved in the culture, knowledge, and civic responsibility we have in our city. Then, if we're worthy, maybe someday we will be remembered too."

Lorenzo appeared suddenly from behind one of the small cloister walls. Because he was still so young, the rigors of study weren't his only daily preoccupations. For him Cosimo was still, and foremost, a playing companion.

"I've finished my exercises! Can we play a little now, Teacher?"

Cosimo and Lorenzo were probably born in a house of Mercato Vecchio, but their first childhood and adolescence memories, except those pertaining to the boarding school, were linked to the house of Piazza Duomo, where they had moved once the family had reached a high financial status.

The two boys had everything. Their father, Giovanni di Bicci, was proud to live at the center of Florence and, in spite of certain austerity norms imposed on the citizens at that time, together with his wife, Piccarda Bueri, he had filled their home with luxury furniture, frescoes, and books.

After all, Giovanni di Bicci had been the true initiator of the family fortune, a savvy businessman capable of exploiting each situation in favor of his own commercial activity. Thanks to his insightful and resourceful spirit, working in the banking system of his uncle Vieri di Cambio de' Medici, Giovanni had quickly moved from the role of apprentice to young associate, managing to establish after the death of Vieri a company of his own, taking over all of the assets and liabilities of the company directed by his uncle.

Giovanni started his career with Vieri with an apprenticeship in the bank's Roman branch, a place of crucial importance due to the presence of the Papal Court. Once there, Giovanni quickly proved his worth as a businessman to the point of being nominated general manager of the branch. Giovanni turned the Roman branch into his own firm and established a long-lasting partnership by sharing the management of the business with a man named Benedetto di Lippaccio de' Bardi.

In October 1397, Giovanni established the head office of his new bank in Florence. This was a timely and clever decision. Although Rome could be regarded as a good source of income because of the financial needs of the pope and all his courtesans and attendants, the real financial heart of Europe was undoubtedly Florence. It was there that the newly founded Medici Bank would have the best chance for investments and financial diversifications.

In a few years, Giovanni's bank and wealth prospered, thanks to his talent in taking advantage of the contacts born out of the work conducted with his uncle, and above all to creating a vast network of branches in Italy and abroad, all connected to the main headquarters in Florence.

When Cosimo and Lorenzo had the chance to spend some time together, they loved to listen to their father's tales, and often Giovanni would linger to tell them about the period he spent working with his uncle, revealing all the secrets of that profession.

"Neither I nor my uncle Vieri were the first Medici to deal

with banks. Several decades ago, some of our ancestors founded the company *Filii Averardi*, or Averardo's Children. They were the sons of Averardo II de' Medici, and there is a bit of my blood in him. One of his children, Salvestro, was my grandfather, but everyone called him Chiarissimo, another of the names and nicknames that appeared many times in the history of our family."

"Is it because of him that our cousin's name is Averardo? In his honor?" asked Lorenzo, referring to Averardo di Francesco di Bicci, son of Giovanni's brother Francesco.

Francesco had worked with Giovanni under Vieri, but at the death of the latter the two brothers founded different banks, and it was indeed Francesco's—the one that Averardo had inherited—with which he was competing with his uncle Giovanni.

"No, boys. Your cousin Averardo is named in honor of his, and your, grandfather. My father."

To trace the history of the *Banco Medici* is to trace the history of business and finance throughout what could be regarded as the formative years of many of the financial institutions existing today.

Over the twelfth and thirteenth centuries, the so-called *Lombardi* or Lombards—the collective noun commonly used to identify bankers from Northern Italy—gradually replaced the Jewish people who historically claimed the role of money lenders to the most powerful and rich families in Europe. The early success of Italian bankers was supported and increased by their business and their introduction of double-entry bookkeeping. This technical innovation, where every transaction was listed in a bank's records in two separate columns, one referring to the debit and the other to the credit side of the company's affairs, greatly increased clarity and could rationalize a company's business decisions: The two columns showed even at a quick glance the nature and profit, or lack thereof, of any transaction and offered a simple way of checking possible inaccuracies or oversights.

Banking was a dangerous profession, not only from a financial point of view, but also because Catholic doctrine punished the sin of usury. Bankers were thus forced to apply a certain degree of creative accounting to their job to avoid the risk of being accused of practicing usury and the interests paid on loans often ended up being recorded either as voluntary gifts or as a reward from the borrower for the risk undertaken by the banker in loaning the money.

"Did you ever consider yourself in danger?" one of the boys now asked Giovanni.

"No, but I did consider myself lucky," said Giovanni. "I was lucky to become part of that world when I was younger. Most of the Northern cities became financial centers—Lucca, Milan, Genoa. But it was Florence that managed to establish itself as the heart of the banking business." Giovanni took a small shining object from his pocket and showed it to his sons. It was a golden coin. "Thanks to this."

It was all due to the solidity of Florence currency—*il fiorino d'oro*, the gold florin that equaled the unchanging quantity of fifty-four grams of gold—as well as the entrepreneurial skills of families such as the Bardi, the Peruzzi, the Acciaiuoli, and, of course, the Medici.

In spite of caring about the boys' training for work since a young age, Giovanni enjoyed making a few digressions, where he described the turbulent times of Florence experienced during his youth, or even told stories his own father told him, like the one about the Black Death epidemic of 1346 that lasted for seven devastating years until 1353, and was considered one of the most shattering catastrophes ever to befall humanity.

Because he was terrified by the plague, it was one of the topics Giovanni discussed more often with his sons, and because a new, albeit less tragic epidemic had struck Florence between April and October 1400.

"I was not even born yet when the great epidemic of 1346 swept through Florence," Giovanni said one day to Cosimo and Lorenzo. "But because I heard so many of my father's stories, I feel like I've been there myself."

"But what can we do about such an illness?" asked Cosimo with uncertainty.

"You must pray to avoid falling sick and, if you do get unwell, pray for a miracle to recover," answered Giovanni. "However, since you have the possibility and the material wealth to do so, you must always give your contribution to Florence each time this terrible sickness should strike the city."

"What happened then? What did grandfather tell you?" asked Cosimo.

"Florence was going through a time of crisis," continued Giovanni. "You already know about the financial and social problems that were afflicting the city. Well, the epidemic made everything worse."

The plague arrived in Europe from China and was carried by Genoese ships that had transited through the ports of the Black Sea. Once struck by the illness, very few people managed to recover, and most of the sick died within three days of the appearance of the first symptoms. Chroniclers of the time reported how the very fabric of European society was torn apart by the plague. Giovanni heard the stories passed down from his own father.

"It was just like the chroniclers said. They wrote that one citizen avoided another, hardly any neighbor troubled about others, relatives never or rarely visited each other . . ."

Lorenzo listened with a flabbergasted, frightened expression. Cosimo held his little brother in his arms to calm him.

Giovanni reminisced about the chronicles from that time. "Moreover, the chroniclers said, such terror was struck into the hearts of men and women by this calamity, that brother abandoned brother, and the uncle the nephew, and the sister her brother, and very often the wife her husband."

By now, Cosimo was getting scared as well. Giovanni had not yet finished his story. "What is even worse and nearly incredible is that fathers and mothers refused to see and tend their children," continued Giovanni, "as if they had not been theirs."

Giovanni wasn't exaggerating. By the end of the epidemic, the plague had wiped out nearly one-third of Europe's population.

Cosimo and Lorenzo were still clinging to each other when Giovanni realized he had scared his sons and leaned over to embrace them.

"I am sorry, children. I didn't mean to frighten you," said Giovanni. "Next time I promise to tell a less scary tale."

But other times his stories were much more interesting and adventurous, as Giovanni also liked to recount tales of illustrious ancestors or relatives whom neither Cosimo nor Lorenzo had never known.

It was Giovanni who told his sons the legend of Charlemagne and of the medicine man. He recounted that story to his sons for the first time in 1400, when the city had been hit by a plague epidemic that had lasted for seven months, from April into October.

"It all started in a small village," he said. "Our ancestors worked as coal men, and maybe some of them were hunters. Mugello was known as the joyous land . . . I am sure they made the best of what they had."

"Do we know the names of these first ancestors?" asked Lorenzo. Giovanni didn't know what to reply to this, but attempted to anyway.

"I knew of a mysterious man, Medico di Potrone, but his story has been lost in time . . ."

Cosimo couldn't resist taking advantage of the occasion to impress his father by reciting de' Rossi's quote. "To not know what came before us is like remaining children forever."

Lorenzo echoed him: "Cicero!"

"Well, I see you're not wasting your teacher's time," concluded Giovanni sardonically.

Cosimo and Lorenzo had heard their father tell that story many times, including a day in 1402, while on their way from home to the *palazzo*, where Giovanni was going after being nominated Priore for the first time. When he came out he found his wife and children waiting for him.

"You're back! Why did you go? You asked them to meet you?" asked Lorenzo impatiently.

"No, I didn't ask them. I waited for the *palazzo* to call me."

"Why is that?" asked Lorenzo.

"Because Nannina suggested me so."

Piccarda loved to hear her nickname on her husband's lips and knew how much Giovanni had been following her advice about not rushing for the race to power.

Piccarda married Giovanni at age eighteen, and was considered to be an extraordinary woman, the ideal Florentine woman of that time: charming, intelligent, observant, and capable of running the household and attending to business during her husband's many absences.

"But you keep listening to your father too," added Piccarda. Cosimo used to listen to both his parents, treasuring those pieces of advice that throughout the years he would follow himself or tell others to follow.

That same year, Cosimo felt his own pride grow even more when he saw his father become one of the judges of the contest for the construction of a new door for the baptistery. Just as it had been for many of their ancestors and as it would be also for Cosimo and the rest of his family, Giovanni knew how to use both art and culture for his own pleasure and personal growth, but also to achieve a position of greater prestige among the citizens.

In occasions like that one, but also by simply meeting him fleetingly in the street, common citizens and eminent members of the city held Giovanni in great esteem.

"A good day to you, *illustrissimo signor* Giovanni!"

"What wonderful furniture you've had built for your home, *caro* Giovanni!"

"Blessed be your union with your wife, and blessed be your children!"

That enthusiasm and love of life, shared among citizens of the most diverse social backgrounds, genuinely embodied the definition of Florence given by Pope Boniface VIII at the end of the thirteenth century, when he said that to the four elements, air, water, earth, and fire, another one should be added: Florentines.

In spite of being one of the richest bankers of Florence, Giovanni remained humble, amused by the stories that were told about his generosity, often made up or exaggerated with easy sentimentalism.

But deep down, Giovanni was satisfied that these stories proved his great popularity. He'd achieved this without rushing in the race for power or an ostentatious display of his wealth and position.

"Thank you for helping my daughter find a good husband. Without a dowry she would have never found anyone!" screamed a woman from her window one day.

A fruit seller gave him a crate of apples picked in the countryside, almost choking up from an undoubtedly made-up story. "This is only a small gift for giving food and shelter to that vagabond child who was selling wood!"

Cosimo knew well his father's noble soul, but he sometimes couldn't come to terms with all that praise heaped on him. "To help everyone, not to hurt anyone" was the maxim that Giovanni used to reply to his son or to anyone else who asked him to explain those occurrences or his acts of generosity.

Piccarda had been described as beautiful among all the women of her time, whereas Giovanni was a man with an average physical appearance, with thick features, bristly hair, eyes far apart from each other, and a large mouth.

He didn't care for his looks, but for all of his life he continued to hone his skills of patience, of cautious but brilliant initiative, of generosity, and of a lack of dangerous ambition. Sometimes, during some moments of domestic tranquility, it was his son who would remind him of his popularity. Giovanni remembered how their ancestors had been treated; these tales were melancholic.

"Like many country people, our family left the Mugello and came down to Florence to settle in the city. At that time, my sons, the peasants who arrived in the city from rural areas in search of fortune, were viewed with contempt."

"It cannot be. No Florentine worthy of this title would treat someone else like this," Lorenzo replied incredulously.

"Yes, it was, Lorenzo. Because at that time, to be a citizen of Florence, born and raised in the city, and maybe even a descendant of ancient Roman families, was a source of great pride. And when someone was an *avventiccio*, meaning a foreigner or simply someone from outside the city, that person was not necessarily treated with respect by many Florentines."

One of these foreigners was certainly Giambuono de' Medici, born between 1130 and 1140, and considered the forefather of the Medici in Florence. A merchant by trade, he probably lived for years in the neighborhood of the Mercato Vecchio, among merchants and commoners. Other traces of Giambuono can be found in a dispute with the Sizi family to obtain the tutelage of Saint Thomas's Church, whose tower had been built with money from both families.

It was in those old streets where the tales would continue, maybe with Piccarda's help, who was as knowledgeable as her husband about the history of Florence.

"What about the Arte? When did our family become part of it?" Cosimo asked one day while in front of the Arte della Lana headquarters, the wool guild, situated behind the church of Orsanmichele.

"Almost since its inception. Our ancestor Chiarissimo, who was related to Giambuono, was a member of this very Arte in front of us and was also part of the *Consiglio Generale della Repubblica*, the General Council of the Republic." Piccarda had answered with the same impetus as her husband and was as proud as he of being a Medici. She spoke about this history as if she had been born into the family itself.

"Was he an important man, then?"

"He was. But he was still part of those *gente nuova*, the new people, whom even people like Dante despised. That was a time when most people thought outsiders were just thinking about gaining *facili guadagni*, easy earnings."

In spite of his being a foreigner and the citizens' mistrust, Chiarissimo prospered as a merchant, she explained.

Even when certain tales of past wrongdoings made him melancholic, consequently worrying Piccarda, to tell of the goals achieved by ancestors like Chiarissimo would make Giovanni proud and happy that his sons knew the family history.

"May the Lord always protect you and your family, most illustrious signor Giovanni!" With the usual deference toward Giovanni and his family members, a member of the Arte della Lana greeted the man at the entrance of the headquarters and, with a broad gesture of his arm, invited them to enter and visit the building.

"And may Saint Thomas always protect you and your enterprise," warmly replied Giovanni, referring to the saint designated as the protector of the wool workers.

The family accepted that invitation with great joy: To be the recipients of such esteem and respect was one of the most desired riches in Florence at the time. Furthermore, in those years Giovanni had started investing capitals outside the bank, and the first two societies he financed were woolen mills.

Around the four visitors, messengers and couriers scurried about, busy with their daily routine between piles of materials, documents, and contracts to fill in. These scenes made Giovanni's eyes twinkle, reminding him of his beloved bank, from which it was hard to leave, even for a single day.

The boys carefully watched, curious not only to learn about the world of business but also from the continuous comings and goings all around, a chaos of sorts that permeated the headquarters.

"The basic rules and duties of each Arte are always the same: Each corporation establishes the price of goods, the manufacturing process, the final quality of the goods, the maximum number of workers for each profession, and, last but not least, the level of the salaries," Giovanni explained. "Remember these things if you want to make good deals when you will be adults."

All the busy people inside the building had different roles and tasks to accomplish. In each Arte, members were generally subdivided between masters—who possessed the raw materials and the tools and who would sell the goods produced in their shops—and apprentices and errand boys.

Moreover, each Arte had a statute that regulated and prescribed severe penalties for those registered members who did not practice the art with the necessary loyalty and honesty, including those who committed fraud concerning the weight and measures in order to earn more, for those who revealed industrial secrets to rival corporations—or worse, to other cities—and who counterfeited the products through any kind of adulteration.

In some extreme cases, the punishment for spilling centuries-old secrets, perhaps concerning a particular kind of wool exclusively produced in Florence, would result in the death of the men or women who revealed them.

Lorenzo observed two errand boys busy carrying wool bales in the small open space at the back of the shop, only to stain them with filthy water and garbage. "It must be unusable material, maybe eaten by mice that probably have also nested inside," explained Giovanni. "In Florence, it is better to destroy goods not up to standards. It would be the stupidest way of ruining a trade."

Giovanni was telling the truth. Goods that had been adulterated or had failed their monthly control because of a poorly calibrated scale, for example, would imply hefty fines, convictions, and probably for the goods in question to be burned publicly. During the night, each corporation had also organized a team of watchmen to monitor their shops, contributing to the safety of their own buildings, and to the general safety of Florence.

After that visit, as they were walking in front of the church of Orsanmichele, which had been for years the chapel of the Arte, Giovanni finished his lesson on the fundamental rules of those corporations.

"We have also had valiant swordsmen, but it was with good judgment that our ancestors made their way in Florence. We wouldn't have otherwise been able to enter the corporations, since their rules were and still are quite rigid—to be an urban or rural Florentine, to be a legitimate child, to provide proof of one's ability in the craft, and to pay the *gravezze*, the taxes, to the municipality. Think how difficult it must have been for an outsider, unless he had great intelligence and competence."

There was another rule that Giovanni was forgetting because it wouldn't have applied to his sons. The rule asked for a "registration tax" to be paid in order to become a member of the Arte, a rule that did not apply to the children of a member of the same Arte.

"It is hard to be a good member of the Arte?" asked Cosimo.

"It is easy to be a good member of the Arte, my sons. Neither more nor less than being a good *guelfo*. And *guelfi* we've always been."

Giovanni was referring to the historical political rivalry between the *guelfi*, followers of the pope, and the *ghibellini*, supporters of the Holy Roman Emperor, which had gripped Florence for centuries, since around 1216, when the population divided itself between Guelphs (*guelfi*) and Ghibellines (*ghibellini*). Giovanni, like all the Medici, had always belonged to the Black *guelfi*, a political faction opposed to the White *guelfi*, and that originally identified itself in the interests of the powerful Donati family.

Not wishing to delve too deeply into these political questions, Giovanni eagerly returned to the discussion of family ancestors.

"Our ancestors were wise merchants, and their skill was evident when they started to take an interest in politics, obtaining positions in the city appointments."

"Were they already well known, like Chiarissimo?"

"So known that they were labeled *la masnada del Mercato Vecchio*, the mob from Mercato Vecchio, and if a man was feared and respected for his skills, people would tell him that he was just like a Medici."

"Do people still say that?"

"Yes, they still do." Giovanni put his hand on the boys' heads. "And they always will."

Chapter Three

RESPONSIBILITIES

When they weren't busy studying, Giovanni personally taught his sons about the bank's activities, explaining the rules and fundamentals of commerce and business. Given the complexity of the financial system at that time, Giovanni had to carefully and patiently prepare the boys.

". . . And every bank works under the same rules dictated by the . . ."

Cosimo was about to repeat some of the last notions he had learned from his father. Giovanni interrupted him. "No, Cosimo, no. You have to understand that all financial institutions are not created the same, and not all of them work under the same regulations and restrictions."

Giovanni knew how banks were organized in Florence during the troubled years of the fourteenth century, when, despite a series of financial and social disasters, the city managed to retain its importance as Europe's financial center with the two new families that took center stage in the banking game: the Pazzi and the Medici.

"You see," he now explained, "each kind of financial activity follows its own set of rules." There were, in fact, four different kinds of banks active at the same time in Florence, each with its own specifications and areas of interest.

"At the bottom of the list, one should place the *banchi di pegno*, the pawn shops," institutions that catered exclusively for the needs of the lowest strata in the population. "They are not even part of the *Arte del Cambio*," remarked Giovanni, mentioning the guild that controlled the banking business in Florence. "But they are under the direct control of the *Signoria*," meaning Florentine government.

The pawnbrokers were initially a mix of Christians and Jews; from 1437, however, the profession remained in the exclusive hands of Jewish brokers, because the Catholic Church considered usury a sin and prohibited Christians to take up such a profession. Although both the Torah and the Hebrew Bible criticized usury, the interpretation of these passages were far from being univocal and Jewish people, who were legally allowed to practice only a few other occupations, were ultimately forced to take up money lending. This historical restriction gave way to a series of negative stereotypes—Jews were regarded as greedy, insolent, prone to taking advantage of others—and created the basis for anti-Semitic propaganda for centuries to come.

"The *banchi di pegno* can charge up to twenty percent of annual interests on loans that are secured against the borrower's properties," added Giovanni. "And you can imagine how dangerous it can get between creditors and debtors."

The religious and social stigma on usury and money lenders was further intensified by what Giovanni mentioned concerning the natural tensions that could develop between creditors (usually Jews) and debtors (very often Christians). Especially in rural areas, poor people who had to pay a large part of their meager earnings to the local lords channeled their discontent toward Jews because they were often in charge of the actual tax collection. In the specific case of Florence, the Catholic Church ban on usury meant that *banchi di pegno* were illegal but they nevertheless managed to survive thanks to a legal loophole or, more precisely, a license fee disguised as penalty: Every year the Florentine government required the collection of a collective fine of 2,000 florins from *banchi di pegno*. Once this fine had been paid, though, the pawnbrokers were safe from the imposition of any further punishment for the sin of usury and were thus free to practice their profession for yet another year.

"Then there's the *banchi a minuto*," continued Giovanni. "These bankers deal with the trade of bullions, the sale of jewels on installment plans, currency exchange, and loans secured by jewels." Such institutions were a sort of retail bank similar to jewelry trading places, and conducted other functions such as granting loans to companies, accepting interest-restricted deposits, or extending monetary assets through payment orders.

"A *banco a minuto* works mainly on the local territory, but major banks like ours do not disdain from working with smaller entities, especially if the business has a good potential," added Giovanni.

By virtue of their intrinsic nature, the *banchi a minuto* were not considered "manifest usurers" and were thus part of the *Arte del Cambio*.

Although historical records on these institutions are scarce, there are traces of time deposits with an interest of about 10 percent, but the surviving ledgers do not report entries related to deposits payable on demand, thus excluding the *banchi a minuto* from the category of deposit banks. Interestingly, there are traces of a limited involvement of the Medici family with two such retail banks, but this happened well after Cosimo's death, between 1476 and 1491, as part of partnerships that dealt heavily with different sorts of luxury goods, from jewels to Spanish tuna.

"What about the *banchi aperti*?" asked Cosimo. *Banchi aperti*, literally "open tables," were another form of banks that were part of the *Arte del Cambio*.

"They are more similar to our activity," replied Giovanni. In fact, the *banchi aperti* were proper transfer and deposit banks, but their peculiarities were to conduct all transactions in public squares and only when the customers were observing. "Even the transfers between two *banchi aperti* are finalized verbally and out in the open," continued Giovanni, and given this unusual way of conducting transactions, the business operations of the *banchi aperti* were characterized by a high degree of risk. By the 1520s, historical records show that only two of them were still operational.

"And then there's us!" exclaimed Lorenzo enthusiastically.

"Yes. We are one of the *banchi grossi*," replied Giovanni. "And one of the biggest in Florence."

The *banchi grossi*, the great banks such as the *Banco Medici*, were the largest financial institutions in Florence. The *banchi grossi* were not just a staple of Florentine economy but, thanks to their vast accumulations of riches and their multifaceted interests, were also the real engine of European economy.

"We are not too dissimilar compared to the *banchi aperti*, though. The main difference between us and them is one of degree rather than kind," added Giovanni.

The *banchi aperti* dealt with all sorts of financial operations, from time deposits to demand and discretionary deposits, and usually diversified their interests by investing in a wide variety of enterprises, while the *banchi grossi* not only reinvested their capital into commercial activities but heavily relied on the emission and circulation of the bills of exchange.

"The bill of exchange is our most important work instrument," ruled Giovanni. "And it is necessary for us in order to transfer the money in places where commerce is conducted with different currencies, or to dispense a credit."

The bill of exchange—*lettera di cambio*—was a notarial act, or an informal letter in other occasions, with which a banker, who had received a deposit from a client, requested from another bank to give back the money to that same person or to carry out a payment. This was probably an Italian invention that preceded by a couple of centuries the Banco Medici, one that then remained essentially unchanged in its form until the eighteenth century. A bill of exchange can thus be defined as the first form of a rudimentary promissory note. The use of bills of exchange allowed not only the movement of capitals from one stock exchange to another, avoiding the more risky physical transportation of cash—a transportation that, even if successful, would have taken at least double the time compared to the letter—but, by carrying out the reimbursement of money lent in another place and in another currency, allowed also to lend money with a high interest rate, bypassing the ban put in place by the Church concerning the sin of usury.

"How does it work?" asked Lorenzo.

"It might sound a little complicated but it's quite simple when you get the gist of it. Now follow me carefully, boys: the *deliverer* in the first city gives money in his own currency to the *taker* and gets from him a bill of exchange in the name of the *payer*, who is the agent of the taker in the second city. The bill of exchange will be in the currency of this second city and will be payable between one and three months to the *payee,* who is the agent of the deliverer in that city. After the collection of the bill, the payee usually buys another bill of exchange in the second city in the name of some merchant working in the first place. This second bill is called *recambium* and is payable with a *usance* of three months to the deliverer in the first city. The second bill of exchange is usually larger than the first sum and its profit derives by the difference in the exchange rates between the two places."

Lorenzo looked at his father, utterly confused.

"Do you understand, Lorenzo?" asked Giovanni.

"I don't think so, Father," replied the boy.

"What about you?" Giovanni asked Cosimo.

"Well, I . . ." Cosimo stuttered.

"It's always complicated the first time! You keep studying hard and gaining experience and you shall comprehend it all, my children!" explained Giovanni.

Very often Giovanni's lessons took place directly at the principal headquarters of the Banco Medici, located close to Orsanmichele, at the crossing between Via Porta Rossa and Via Calimala.

Giovanni's associate, Benedetto di Lippaccio de' Bardi, was always there to welcome them. The two men were not only linked by business, but by an old friendship and the satisfaction of having succeeded together.

"Giovanni, you old war horse! I was starting to think you were too tired to come to work today!" started off Benedetto with a roaring tone of voice.

"You're not young yourself anymore, Benedetto!" replied Giovanni. "Unlike Cosimo and Lorenzo here."

"Is your father still behaving, boys, or has old age finally got to his head?" pressed on an amused Benedetto.

"Will you stop being a nuisance and help me with the daily business, please?" asked a resigned though equally amused Giovanni.

"Our world is pure madness, but you'll soon learn to love it," said Benedetto, addressing the boys.

The parent company of the Banco Medici exuded even more of that feeling of controlled chaos that Cosimo and Lorenzo had experienced during their visit to the headquarters of the Arte della Lana.

While he was teaching the boys, Giovanni stopped himself from giving directives to his employees or letters to the clerks, who alternatively would drown him in a flood of questions about this or that matter.

"What about the wool shipment to London, signor Giovanni?"

"The price of the goods departing for France has been devalued!"

"An English emissary who wishes to ask information on the Arte della Seta is galloping here from the road of . . ."

"One at a time, one at a time!" yelled Benedetto, trying in vain to keep the employees from surrounding Giovanni.

During rare moments of calm, Giovanni would manage to resume the lessons in his office, where, at least until the arrival of new duties, he continued to provide rules and advice to his children.

"This is our fortress, boys. From our parent company you

will steer the direction of its business, and it will almost always be from here that you will receive news and give instructions."

"Giovanni, the English emissary is about to arrive," intervened Benedetto, resigned to not being able to give even a few moments of peace to his associate.

Giovanni continued, knowing that he had to welcome the emissary in a few minutes. "You are already surrounded by excellent collaborators," he said, pointing to Benedetto. "But just like me, they won't be eternal, and you will have to use your shrewdness to find some equally valuable ones of your own." From the street could be heard the shuffling of at least three horses' hooves, a sign that the Englishman and his collaborators had arrived.

Giovanni tried to conclude: "Moreover, to always receive precise news you will have to maintain good relationships with the rulers of each country, with the aristocratic houses, and with all those that may be of use to you in business, but . . ."

"But?" asked Lorenzo, uncertain about that sentence left to linger dramatically.

"Don't always trust kings and other nobility, because they are often the ones who don't pay!" replied Giovanni. "Do you remember the company Filii Averardi?"

"What happened to them?" asked Cosimo.

"Let's say that the dissolution of the company was an act of Godly mercy, because it prevented it from going bankrupt like the banking groups of the Bardi, those of the Peruzzi or the Acciaiuoli . . ."

"You mean that . . ."

"Yes, that the then-English sovereign forgot to pay back the loans he had taken for the war he was fighting!" exclaimed Giovanni, referring to the insolvency of Edward III, who was incapable of repaying the enormous loans taken from the

Florentine banks to finance the Hundred Years' War against France. The insolvency of the sovereign had caused a crisis for even a tested system like the Florentine one, causing the equivalent of a disastrous downfall of the stock exchange of today, capable of sending into bankruptcy the most important banks of the city, including the one belonging to the family of Cosimo's future wife.

All of a sudden Giovanni became more serious. In a voice full of both enterprise and caution, he added, "My sons, my tales about our past activities may have amused you, but remember—never underestimate our place in the world." His voice had become full of pride. "We and a few other cities are at the center of international commerce. We have undisputed control over the Mediterranean and our merchants dominate the trade of spices, silk, wool, and cloth from the Orient. But what makes us better than everyone else is that our businessmen and merchants can rely on a banking system that is the most efficient and successful in Europe. Tell me, children, what is our profession?"

"Bankers," answered the boys.

"Yes, but not completely correct. We aren't simple bankers who merely deal with day-to-day activities like pawn broking and money changing. We have the monopoly over foreign banking, and that means dealing in bills of exchange and . . ."

Benedetto was forced to once more interrupt his associate's discourse: "Giovanni, I'm afraid I have to tell you that . . ."

". . . The Englishman has arrived. Yes, I understand," Giovanni sadly replied, and he took his leave from the boys with a gentle stroke on their heads, and one last sentence. "You will learn, my sons."

But in addition to Cosimo's primary responsibilities of studying and the bank, he soon had another.

Sometime after, on a day in 1406 when he was seventeen, the boy learned that he'd been charged with an unexpected duty. Upon returning home, Cosimo found his father waiting for him with another man. It was Gino Capponi, an influential politician, member of the Dieci della Guerra (a war council composed of ten people) and the most trusted right-hand man, together with Niccolò da Uzzano, of Maso degli Albizzi.

"Sit down, my son. There is something we must discuss," started Giovanni.

Capponi took the floor. His tone was martial, his demeanor the one of a man both feared and respected. After all, he was a man who had been capable of climbing back on the ladder of power after falling into extreme poverty during the Ciompi Uproar.

Capponi also knew how to adapt to war, a virtue that in those times of struggles between cities was quite respected, on top of being well remunerated. During the Renaissance, war was an art as well, and the Italians were its most talented artists.

"It appears Pisa has finally capitulated. It's another glorious day for Florence. Now it's time for treaties, agreements, and precautions," said Capponi, stressing the last word. "Do you understand what that means, Cosimo?"

"I do," replied Cosimo without hesitating.

"Very well, then. Your father will arrange everything necessary. I must go now. We'll be departing soon, along with my son and the other hostages. Don't worry, it won't be for long, as Pisa wants to sign every treaty much faster than we do."

To exchange hostages as a precaution, to allow the negotiations at the end of a conflict between cities to unfold without betrayals and cheap shots, was a custom of the time, but it was the first time that Cosimo had been chosen to be one of the hostages.

It wasn't that big a surprise, as children from rich and powerful families were brought up knowing their duties, but on his part Cosimo was disappointed at the prospect of interrupting his training for goodness knows how long. Moreover, even if those exchanges were routine, the hatred that existed between the two cities was such that the situation could always present an unforeseen event or bad surprise. Giovanni tried to cheer him up with some slightly macabre humor.

"I guess it's not the best time to tell you about our ancestor Giovanni, who was executed about a century ago during a war against Lucca . . ."

Cosimo looked at him without replying. What was decided by those who governed Florence was law, and the boy would not dare to go against a decision that, if refused, could have created problems not only for his father, but for the whole family as well.

Giovanni sighed, trying to raise the morale of the son ready to do his duty for Florence but saddened for having to cease, even temporarily, his studies and the apprenticeship at the bank.

"I'm sorry, Cosimo. You will go back to your books and your work as soon as you return. And with your mother keeping an eye on me and your little brother, the bank won't disappear. Don't worry."

Giovanni was certainly mortified that his son was forced to interrupt his training, but he was also proud that Cosimo would be one of the hostages of prestige, among whom were chosen the descendants of the most illustrious families of the city.

That expansionist war was only the newest chapter in the centuries-old conflict with Pisa; it wasn't the first one fought by

Florence and it wouldn't be the last. Pisa had forever been one of Florence's long-standing rivals, and in 1260, in a coalition with Siena and Terni, with Manfred, King of Sicily, and with other allies, had severely defeated the Florentines during the battle of Montaperti, a tragic moment in the history of the city and of the centuries-old fight between the *guelfi* and the *ghibellini*.

Once the power had been reclaimed and the old institutions reestablished, thanks to the victory in battle, the *ghibellini* decreed a series of retaliations that included the exile, goods confiscation, and destruction of the *guelfi*'s estates.

Only the death of Manfred in 1266, killed in battle by Charles I of Anjou, who had become the new King of Sicily, as well as Farinata degli Uberti's impassioned defense, a *ghibellino* but a true Florentine who did not want to see his own city annihilated, had saved Florence from destruction. Born shortly after the time of the battle in 1265, Dante Alighieri would insert Farinata in his *Divine Comedy* in the tenth *canto* of hell, among the epicurean heretics, also remembering his determining role in saving Florence from being wiped out.

Giovanni tried to express his appreciation for his son's stoic will and desire to do his duty for Florence by referring precisely to this event.

"For six long years, Florence was exposed to the risk of being leveled to the ground, just as it happened during antiquity," Giovanni said with seriousness.

"I don't understand why someone would destroy Florence instead of taking it and its riches," replied Cosimo, his pragmatic mentality at work even in analyzing wars and plunders.

"Don't be surprised by how strange the desire a man in search of his own satisfaction can be."

"Do only enemies have this kind of desire?" asked Cosimo.

"No, Cosimo. Unfortunately, it happens also to friends. And we always have to be careful that this doesn't happen to ourselves," concluded Giovanni with a tinge of bitterness. "Now, go say goodbye to your mother and brother. They will miss you terribly. I know I will."

A few days after, Gino Capponi was marching toward Pisa. He had been among the main architects of the victory in the conflict, so much so that he became the first governor of the conquered city, but the siege had been long and costly for the enemy. Outside Pisa's gates, his gaze crossed the official who was accompanying the hostages from Pisa to Florence, and Cosimo noticed the harsh but tired eyes of the two men of war. Meanwhile, another old man of war, a Florentine official of Capponi's bodyguards, had started to swear.

"Cursed Pisans! For centuries we've clashed with them and we'll still do it hundreds of years from now!"

Another soldier echoed him. "You can starve them, and you can threaten to hang them all, yet they won't surrender!"

"Quit complaining for now and act like the soldiers you are," ordered Capponi, who was feared and respected by his men.

"Don't worry, my father says everything will be all right." Neri Capponi, son of Gino, intervened to calm and distract Cosimo and the other younger hostages from those conversations.

"My father says it too."

This time the voice was the one of Luca degli Albizzi, son of the very powerful Maso. Cosimo made a sign of agreement directed at the two boys. He did not yet know that one day Luca would become one of his few allies while going against his brother Rinaldo, nor that Neri would have been a mediator between the two families during the period when Cosimo would be exiled. On that day, the citizens of Florence were only thinking about the end of hostilities against Pisa, and maybe about future triumphs.

Cosimo and the other hostages lived comfortably in Pisa but the risk of imminent danger and the constant watching behind their backs took a mental toll on some of those young minds, feeding their paranoia for many years to come.

Others, such as Cosimo, fared better, learning and maturing from the experience.

"Cosimo's back! Cosimo's back!" shouted Lorenzo when, a few weeks later, his older brother returned home, escorted by elite soldiers of the Signoria, who guaranteed the safe passage of every hostage to Florence. As Giovanni stood on the threshold watching his older son dismount from a horse, Piccarda and Lorenzo rushed to hug Cosimo.

"Florence will remember your deed," whispered Piccarda.

"Never go away that long again or I'll ask them to keep you forever," prompted Lorenzo. Cosimo looked at his father and they exchanged a nod. It was time to get back to business and study, and if Giovanni couldn't wait to resume mentoring his son, Cosimo couldn't wait to learn more either.

Time passed, and the two boys were growing up. Cosimo had an increasingly clear picture of what his future would be made of, while Lorenzo was becoming almost as capable as his brother.

Giovanni had many years of great gratification, not only because of the success of the bank and other commercial ventures, but because of the public career that sent him on diplomatic missions as governor of the city of Pistoia or, on three occasions, in charge of fulfilling the role of prior of the Arte del Cambio.

In 1414, when Cosimo was twenty-five, he accompanied his

father on a diplomatic mission to Bologna, where Giovanni had met a man known several years before when he was still working in Rome, someone who had become an odd combination of friend and client. This man was Baldassarre Cossa, known to future generations as the Antipope John XXIII for his opposition to the pope chosen by the Catholic Church.

Those were turbulent years for religion. As a matter of fact, between the second half of the fourteenth century and the beginning of the fifteenth, the Church was going through a period of crisis, called the Great Western Schism, which lasted almost forty years in a clash between popes and antipopes for the control of the pontifical throne.

In 1414, three reigning popes contended for the keys to Saint Peter: Gregory XII in Rome, Benedict XIII in Avignon, and the aforementioned John XXIII in Pisa. The latter probably dedicated himself to an ecclesiastical career more to follow his family's wish than as a true vocation. According to historical witnesses, his true talents lay in political ambition, tactical skills in military matters, and the ability to administer power. All of these characteristics, together with his love of women, made him a figure closer to a *condottiero* or mercenary captain than a man of faith.

Even considering his caution and perspicacity in judging others, Cosimo's father had decided to support an individual as controversial as the antipope, starting a long-lasting friendship as his personal banker. This was also done in order to exploit Cossa's position, which, had he managed to become pope, would have made it possible for the Medici Bank to become one of the main papal banks, dedicated to the managing of the curia. This did occur in 1410, though Cossa was still contending the scepter with his other two rivals.

❦

There was a reason why Giovanni brought Cosimo with him, and riding in a cart on their way back home he expressed his motivations.

"Is your mind busy, my son?" asked Giovanni to Cosimo, as he was distracted watching the countryside pass before his eyes.

"A little, Father," answered the young man.

"As always!" exclaimed Giovanni.

"Where am I needed when we return?" asked Cosimo.

"With your soon-to-be wife, of course. We'll start the preparations for the wedding as soon as possible," announced Giovanni.

This piece of news made Cosimo rejoice—he hoped his wedding would be a holy union like the one between Giovanni and Piccarda. Though he did not say it out loud, Cosimo's father was hoping that this event would also increase the number of his prominent friendships even more.

"Of course, it might take a few months to prepare the big event," continued Giovanni.

"How so, Father?" asked Cosimo.

"I'll tell you . . ." replied Giovanni, and then added obscurely, "But first tell me, Cosimo, do you think about ambition? Not what you discussed with your tutors, but concerning your life, your career?"

Cosimo thought about it for a moment. He knew he could speak freely with his father, but hesitated slightly as if he feared to appear too arrogant. "I want to follow great ambitions, Father," he said eventually. "Because I think that to have small ones means to lag behind and be considered as someone mediocre in the city."

The words of Cosimo were certainly not dictated by arrogance or by a sudden change of character, but simply his seriousness and attachment to his studies and work.

Giovanni hesitated as well before replying. He wanted to express his words in the best possible way to make Cosimo understand that what he was about to tell him was a decision for his own good.

"There is a lot of talk in the city about you, my son," began Giovanni. "And everyone says that you distinguish yourself for your seriousness and that you only spend time with people of virtue, who are alien to carelessness or distractions."

Cosimo seemed satisfied, though not too surprised, by those words.

Giovanni continued. "And they say that you do not tolerate buffoons, melodramatic people, or those who spend their time uselessly. Is it true?"

"It is, father," replied Cosimo.

"But there is something you don't know or that you don't fully understand," continued Giovanni. "You have to know, my son, that there is a weed that can grow in every garden, a weed one shouldn't water but let it go dry. This weed is envy."

Giovanni knew quite a bit about ambition, especially the extent to which it can attract envy, and Florence at that time could well be a garden where negative feelings could grow luxuriant, watered by the political and social conditions of the city.

"The more this weed is wicked, Cosimo," added Giovanni, "the more difficult it is to eliminate. This is why we must be careful that it doesn't grow too much."

After all, Cosimo aroused envy in all of his peers, especially Rinaldo, Maso's son, who was less educated and less gifted than Cosimo, but anxious to measure himself against his rival. Maso wasn't dead yet, but Rinaldo was already looking toward the future, and he had already thought about having Cosimo banished from the city with the accusation of being a danger for the Republic.

Niccolò da Uzzano was firmly opposed to this plan, fearing that the struggle between the two young men would make a despot of the winner, affirming, "May God prevent any of them from becoming a tyrant to our city."

The cart transporting father and son was jumping up and down because of the many stones scattered on the road. Giovanni picked up the hat that had fallen after one particularly hard bump and continued his explanation by remembering a past episode. "I was just a young man when I saw my cousin Salvestro triumphantly carried during the Ciompi Uproar. For the *popolo minuto* to be denied even their fundamental rights is something my cousin couldn't stand for."

It was true. Salvestro was a man who had already fulfilled important public posts, but he could not tolerate the injustices and reactionary behavior that the *guelfi* and art-consuls had assumed, attached as they were to an obsolete conservative behavior and incapable of addressing the social demands of that time.

"I could not have tolerated certain injustices myself, Father," replied Cosimo.

"I know, but there is more to this story. In 1378, when it became known that Salvestro would become Gonfaloniere di Giustizia, this cheered up the *ciompi*, while various representatives of the *guelfi* tried to prevent the election, not succeeding in their intent," continued Giovanni. "But they continued to go against him, and sabotaged his work when he proposed a law against the magnates. It was then that Salvestro threatened to resign, provoking the *ciompi* uprising. Several houses of *guelfi* families were burned and there was extensive damage to the city while Salvestro's law was being approved in a heated climate."

"What happened then?" asked Cosimo.

"Because of the Signoria's indignant reaction, Salvestro resigned from his post so as not to interfere against the rebels. He then retired to private life, but continued to have the esteem of the people, becoming the personal adviser to Michele di Lando, the poor wool comber who had become the *ciompi* leader. Subsequently, Michele became the new *gonfaloniere*, advised by Salvestro himself."

"But things took a wrong turn," anticipated Cosimo.

"Yes, it's true, things took a wrong turn. The *ciompi* found themselves with too much power and too soon. They didn't know how to keep what they had conquered, nor how to use it wisely. And my cousin understood that the moment to suppress that uproar he had worked so hard for had arrived, even though it had begun for the right reasons. Do you remember what happened to him?"

"I only know that he died shortly before I was born," said Cosimo.

"In spite of Salvestro having done everything in his power to set right that situation that had gotten out of control, in the end he paid for his faults and was exiled by the Albizzi with the accusation of having exercised tyranny over the population. Do you understand why I have told you this story and what it means?"

Cosimo didn't reply, letting his father continue talking.

"It means that the people would be ready to follow someone like you, but also that every man can easily make mistakes and fall into temptation, no matter how righteous he may be, or how fair the cause he is embracing." With a more serious tone

63

he added, "That's why I've decided you will leave the city for at least a year. It's not your time to fight any battles for the citizens, and you have to stay away from the *palazzo* and its temptations. When you return, you will know more of how the world works, and will have given the time for the envy some people feel for you to cool. And, of course, we will see to your marriage as soon as you set foot back in Florence."

Indeed, in this time, momentary separations between husbands and wives (as well as soon-to-be married couples) were normal, and could last months or even years; in the big banking and merchant families it was often a matter of journeys with business interests tied to international markets, and no head of family devoted to his business would have second thoughts about splitting a couple, even right after the wedding.

"I have already traveled a lot for the bank's business and for my studies, Father. But if you deem this necessary, then I will do it. Where am I to go?"

"There is an important deed that seems tailored for your talents, and it concerns my friend Baldassarre Cossa," said Giovanni.

"What is it about?" asked Cosimo.

"You will know when it's time," replied Giovanni sardonically. "And the key concerning your part is in here." He took out an envelope that Cossa had given him during their meeting in Bologna.

The cart driver halted the horses abruptly after a last big shake. He turned toward father and son.

"Is there some kind of problem? Did one of the wheels split?" asked Giovanni.

"Florence is in sight, signor Giovanni," replied the driver, shaking his head in reply to the question. "And one can already feel we're home."

Chapter Four

TRAVELING THE ALPS

It was the end of September 1414 and in a few months, in the city of Constance in Germany, an ecumenical council would take place in order to put an end to the Great Western Schism.

With fewer than ten thousand inhabitants, Constance was about to host a great number of guests, including hundreds of church personalities. The communal councils found themselves faced with the necessity of having to provide food and shelter, plus taking care of all of the participants' other needs, including the accessibility and availability of bank services the way the men of the curia were used to.

Before the council, there were no Italian banks in Constance, and even if the local merchants were well established on the international market and were also working with the Florentine banks using the usual bills of exchange, no one had direct ties or great familiarity with the payment system used by the curia.

It was to address these necessities that the organizers of the council invited the major Italian banks to open branches in the city, so as to guarantee, almost always at the request of the same invited banks, that the branches would not be subjected to the local laws and regulations but would conduct their business as an Italian enclave in a foreign country.

Obviously, because of its importance, capability, and ties with one of the three popes, the Banco Medici had been among the first companies to receive the invitation. Even more so, given the enormous amount of business deals that it managed for the pontiff, the bank had to divide its work into two branches: one based in Rome and the other as a "mobile bank" ready to follow the pontifical court in each and every one of its travels.

Paradoxically, until a few years before, it would have been unthinkable for Giovanni to consider a business journey in Germany. Indeed, at the beginning of the Banco Medici, Giovanni had inserted a clause in each contract that forbid his business partners and employees to grant loans or do business with German merchants or businessmen.

He did not trust their banking organization, which he considered outdated and unreliable compared to the Italian one. He had been particularly burned when the director of the Venetian branch of the Banco Medici, Neri Tordaquinci, tried to hide having loaned money to some German merchants, who then ran away without reimbursing the sum, by modifying ad hoc the accounting records.

Times had changed, though, and so had the necessity of continuously expanding in order to continue to do business with success. Giovanni had the utmost trust in his son's abilities and wanted him to lead the Medici company to Germany, while accompanied by Lorenzo and a few other trusted men.

On top of the wish to remove Cosimo from Florentine

envy, Giovanni genuinely considered that such a journey could develop his professional qualities as well as his human ones, just as he had told his son during their return trip from Bologna.

Besides, Giovanni also wanted someone he could blindly trust to control the expenditures made by Cossa, who shortly before had asked for, and obtained, an enormous loan from Giovanni, far bigger than the already sizable ones he often asked of the Banco Medici.

"Do you remember the envelope that I had shown you during our last trip?" said Giovanni to Cosimo while he was showing him the contents of said document. "It is a papal safe conduct pass that will allow you to reach Constance safely."

"How long do you think the council will last, Father?" asked Cosimo.

"It's a thorny question, but I trust that it will be solved quickly, for Christianity's sake," said Giovanni with a tone that couldn't hide some uncertainty, but then he concluded with a joke. "And I wouldn't want to go back on the promise of organizing the preparations for your wedding and your brother's—so please be safe."

"Young men with your talents are always needed somewhere," said Piccarda while she was helping her sons prepare their luggage for the trip. "And I know you will do justice to our family and our activity this time as well."

"We will come back soon, Mother," said Lorenzo.

"When you come home, you will bring two joys to your father and me—your return and your weddings," replied Piccarda.

Cosimo and Lorenzo took their leave from their mother with an embrace. "Keep making us proud," said their mother, then adding, full of love, "Now go, the pope is waiting for you."

Once the preparations finished, Cosimo and Lorenzo left for Germany together with Ilarione de' Bardi—brother of Benedetto, Giovanni's longtime associate—and Poggio Bracciolini and Leonardo Bruni, both great historians and humanists at the service of John XXIII, respectively as *secretarius domesticus* (responsible for redacting the private correspondence of the pontiff) and pontifical secretary.

Bracciolini and Bruni were held in high esteem by both Giovanni and Cosimo: the two were indeed perfect examples of brilliant men of letters, capable of putting themselves at Florence's service as public officials of the utmost integrity, in the wake of the teachings of Coluccio Salutati, an important politician and figure of Florentine humanism, who had also influenced Roberto de' Rossi, Cosimo and Lorenzo's tutor.

Cosimo admired the two men, especially for their personal talents, like the capacity and dedication of Bracciolini in search-ing for presumably lost classics of Latin literature, or Bruni's knowledge of Greek literature, the language which he was one of the first Florentine humanists to master.

Preceding the group on the road to Constance was Cossa himself, who for personal safety reasons was taking the trip with the protection of numerous soldiers and bodyguards.

Even with the safe conduct pass provided by Cossa, crossing the Alps was a long and strenuous journey. The only moments of distraction for the five men and their escorts (a small group of bodyguards, employees of the bank, and scholars; nothing com-pared to the numbers of Cossa's procession) were the stops at the roadside for food and drink at various inns. The men rested for a few hours at these intervals before resuming the journey on uneven paths and poorly connected roads.

Between a bowl of hot soup and a cup of watered-down

wine, Cosimo often took advantage of these little pauses to exchange opinions and jokes with his travel companions.

"Did you make your will, Ilarione?" began Cosimo, with a pinch of that taste for macabre jokes that he probably inherited from his father.

"Given how often I travel, it is always in the drawer of my writing desk. It is pointless to make a new version each time, don't you think?" exclaimed Ilarione, who then added in a playful tone, "And you? What will your future wife think about this absence? Maybe that you are already fed up with her and that you don't want to marry her?"

"What could she possibly think?" intervened Leonardo Bruni. "Except that until someone grants wings to mankind, neither the dangers nor the necessary time for a similar journey will ever change."

"Wings! I understand that man should always try to obtain what he has not, but this would be too much," exclaimed an amused Ilarione.

All of those utterances were based on reality. Just as much as separating couples, even Cosimo's joke about drafting one's will before departing was really a consistent routine for every traveler, because the roads to travel by horse were still full of dangers.

Like all the travelers of their time and especially those who worked in commerce or in the banks, Cosimo and his comrades knew well of the risks that they ran during a long journey. The danger of the roads was another reason why there had been the diffusion of the bill of exchange, so as to avoid the danger of attracting too much undesired attention in the transportation of great riches while traveling.

Poggio Bracciolini had his say while shifting the conversation away toward a more intellectual subject. "It wouldn't be a bad thing to take advantage of the time we will spend in Constance to also look for rare books. We could try to look not only on the German territory, but also in France." Then he added with some good-natured irony, "What do you say about it, Cosimo? Or do you perhaps have too many volumes to read in your personal library?"

"This will never happen—having too many books is impossible!" readily replied Cosimo. "And I also say that such distractions would make this journey a real pleasure as well as a duty." He massaged his back, tired after several hours of travel, and added with a chuckle, "And a duty that until now revealed itself as something rather uncomfortable."

The proposal submitted by Bracciolini was obviously extremely interesting for Cosimo, who, once everyone's laughter for his joke went quiet, added right away: "What do you hope to find with this new research, Bracciolini? Did you get some useful clues from your usual contacts?"

To that question Bracciolini's face brightened. "I am confident that I will be able to find something in the abbeys and convents of the cities around Constance. My sources told me that the presence of several Latin pieces of literature, which have never been transcribed or made known, is to be taken for granted."

"Maybe study books for children or on how to cook for a whole Roman legion," joked Ilarione, then observing, "Your pursuit is noble but should only be aimed at texts that are useful."

Cosimo intervened. "I am surprised about the lightheartedness of your sentence, Ilarione. Just as one can't have too many books, in the same way there can never be useless books, especially if they come from such a remote and important past."

Ilarione lowered his head, understanding that he had crossed the line with his joke, even if he meant no harm. Then Cosimo added, "Do you think that Bracciolini could choose which books fate allows him to find and rediscover for humanity?"

Bracciolini concluded his argument with enthusiasm: "Maybe one of these abbeys could even hide some unknown text of Cicero or Quintilian. Wouldn't it be incredible?"

"We have a lot to do, but we pray that we will have enough time, even for only one day," replied Cosimo. With sincere admiration he said, "And I would be honored if you accepted me to accompany you in this new quest."

"You have spoken well, my brother," Lorenzo interrupted with a more pragmatic tone of voice. "We really have a lot to do to install our branch there, and I wonder how much time will we effectively be able to put aside for more pleasant distractions."

"To risk outstanding sums for uncertain financial benefits only to please some high-ranking prelate? Could it be old age playing tricks with my mind or is it that as time passes your Medici acuity is going feeble? I would not have expected it from a mind like yours," teased Leonardo Bruni with sarcasm. He was the oldest member of the group.

Lorenzo got the joke right away and replied in the same spirit. "Such a sentence from an ex-chancellor of our republic and current pontifical secretary? Your revered age aside, we are the ones who would never expect that life and its experiences could harden you this much, Leonardo!"

There was an explosion of laughter among the travelers; Cosimo looked at his brother, happy to see how much Lorenzo had become shrewd and quick with his words.

Lorenzo continued more seriously. "You are right,

nevertheless. It is because of this that we have demanded, and received, a certain number of privileges from the emperor, from the city, as well as from the ecclesiastical councils. Isn't it, Ilarione?"

Ilarione nodded and confirmed what Lorenzo said. "It is true, what we have asked for has been given to us without opposition." He started to list the various conditions obtained: "The Banco Medici branch will not be submitted to local corporate or judicial regulations, nor will it be limited by customs' taxes and duties. We have also obtained the permission to export gold, silver, and other valuables without any limits."

"It is normal for a bank like the one of the Medici to receive these attentions," added Bracciolini.

"But maintaining the high standards which allow us to receive them is our duty as well," said Cosimo. "And, in any case, it is about attentions obtained by all of the other banks that will be present at the council."

After several days of travel, the group had finally arrived in Constance, shortly preceded by Cossa and his entourage.

All of Constance was buzzing with excitement; its roads and houses were full of visitors. Between religious people, bankers, and knights with respective personal followings, the city had welcomed at least forty thousand guests, more than three times its population.

Arriving at the end of their long journey, Cosimo and his comrades were immediately greeted by a rival administrator. "Here are the *mercatores florentini romanam curiam sequentes*," exclaimed the man using the Latin formula to define those bankers who took care of the curia's business.

That administrator had been sent there by the bank of

Averardo, cousin of Cosimo and Lorenzo and son of Giovanni's brother. His name was Andrea di Lippaccio de' Bardi, and he was one of Benedetto and Ilarione's brothers.

"It seems like everyone is here," said Lorenzo, surveying the crowd.

"Everyone, but only if we count the most important of our profession," replied Andrea.

"Also counting family reunions," said Ilarione while greeting his brother.

Taking a look around, Cosimo recognized many familiar faces. "I have seen people representing the Alberti, the de' Ricci, and several others," he said. "So much work generates a huge business turnover."

"Let's hope so," replied Andrea. "But I heard rumors that claim we will soon leave the region, so much so that no one wanted to buy a house. We have all rented places to sleep and work in."

"And I imagine that with these rents, the wealthy people of this city will become even more wealthy," intervened Ilarione.

"That's a good guess, brother," replied the administrator. "But those who will earn the most in the end will still be ourselves."

As predicted, the following months were full of work for the Banco Medici and all of the other financial companies that were present in the area. To this day the available written sources concerning the business activities conducted during the Council of Constance is enormous: accounting, administrative, and council documents are only a small testimony of the real amount of work conducted by Cosimo and his colleagues during the brief existence of these Italian branches on German territory.

In the comfort of the house they had rented from a rich

merchant, Cosimo and Lorenzo often found themselves in conversations with Ilarione about the quantity and quality of work they were carrying out.

"Keep reporting the expenses on the accounts notebook, Ilarione. The report we have to send back to Florence must be as precise as possible," said Cosimo. "And don't forget to separate the expenses pertaining to the bank from the daily ones."

"I am doing this already," replied Ilarione. "I am using purposefully separate papers to mark down daily expenses."

"Which entries have you included?" asked Lorenzo.

"Obviously, the rent of the house and the payments to the locals we hired, like the servants, cooks, and messengers," replied Ilarione. "The same for the money spent for food and for those objects of daily use."

Lorenzo took a look at the papers, and was impressed by Ilarione's precision. "You have also divided the expenditures for food and goods in different sections, according to whether they have been bought by German or Italian merchants."

Ilarione laughed and added, "There is even a column to separate our fellow citizens from other Italian merchants. Far too many Florentines have arrived here to do business with the council. May their knack for profit always be blessed!"

"Even only in terms of meticulousness you are worthy of your brother Benedetto, Ilarione!" said an equally impressed Cosimo.

Lorenzo took the papers pertaining to the bank transactions in his hands. "Bills of exchange and the granting of credits. I never guessed we could make plenty of business of this kind and practically none in terms of activity of goods selling."

Cosimo replied promptly, "Here our services are in demand for other things rather than buying or selling goods."

That reply perfectly outlined how the banking sector had become an essential extension for the pontifical state, which was now using banks to manage its various forms of income.

The incomes would become part of the Church's intake from various sources: exotic goods coming from the most remote dioceses of Europe were to be converted into money, the selling of ecclesiastical appointments inside the curia and the selling of indulgences were to receive a papal dispensation for any kind of sin. There was also a market for selling relics of saints, including cases of their limbs or heads.

The groups of bankers wouldn't spend too much time caring for socializing, either with their German landlords or between each other, and they would only meet on rare occasions, often to coincide with religious ceremonies in the city church. During such events, Cosimo and the others sometimes met with the administrator of Averardo's bank.

"Where are your scholar friends?" asked Andrea, referring to Poggio Bracciolini and Leonardo Bruni.

"At the service of the pope and busy with their research—duties and pleasures less worldly than ours," replied Cosimo.

"You enjoy an excellent reputation as a scholar and passionate man of letters, Cosimo. Haven't you taken time to spend with them in these less worldly activities?" asked Andrea.

"You know how busy we are because of the commitments of our work, but there will be occasions," replied Cosimo.

"I hope so for yourself, but maybe it won't be here in Constance. I keep thinking that we will soon go back to our homes," added the man.

"We will go back home as soon as the *pacem, exaltationem et reformationem ecclesiae, ac tranquillitatem populi cristiani* is reached," concluded Cosimo, quoting the Latin sentence used by the organizers to open the council and establish the goals to reach during its duration—peace, the exaltation and reform of the Church, and tranquility for Christians.

The administrator was wrong about the length of the council. It was prolonged until 1418, managing during the course of several months to depose all of the three popes and elect a new one, Martin V, charged with managing the last months of the council from November 1417 until its conclusion in April 1418.

In spite of solving the issue involving the three popes, before the election of Martin V, the council had set for him the goal of reforming the Church from the inside by changing its constitution and suppressing most of the centralization of power. Another goal was to fight the way members of the curia and clergy lived and prospered through frivolousness and indiscipline. In spite of these intentions, the contrasting opinions and the struggle for power remained entrenched, and an agreement was reached only on a few points.

Feeling cornered, Baldassarre Cossa tried to run away from Constance in 1415. But after returning to the city by force, and after a long negotiation, he was pushed to abdication. The Banco Medici group left again for Florence after Cossa's abdication, and due to the agreements previously made with the German authorities, Cosimo and his partners encountered no problems during their journey back, in spite of their worries and apprehensions.

Tired from the long period of stress and work in Constance, the travelers resumed their usual conversations to ease the tediousness on the road home. At the table of an inn where they stopped to enjoy a frugal meal, Cosimo seemed pensive, while clutching in his hands a letter, still closed, that had arrived shortly before from Florence.

"Poor Bruni and Bracciolini, servants of a pope who is no more," ruled Ilarione while observing Bruni, who was sadly eating his dinner on his own, away from the others.

"Men and scholars like them always find an occupation worthy of their reputation," replied Cosimo, as the sentence Piccarda uttered while saying goodbye to her sons came back to his mind.

"After this event, I think Bruni will permanently move to Florence," said Lorenzo.

"And will probably ask for its citizenship," added Cosimo.

"I didn't think Bracciolini would remain in Constance," said Ilarione.

"He took a wise decision," replied Cosimo. "On top of wanting to wait for the council's new decision and find a potential new occupation with the new pope, Bracciolini will now also have much more time to dedicate to his research of lost classical works."

"And to think that I had joked about his possibilities of finding time for his research," exclaimed Ilarione.

"When we said goodbye, he told me he had located two of Cicero's orations," added Cosimo. "And that soon he will explore the Swiss convents and cathedrals in search for works by his beloved Quintilian."

"You think he will find them?" asked Lorenzo.

"As I said, men like him always find something," replied Cosimo.

While the others had resumed eating, Cosimo had opened the letter that had reached him from home. Contessina had sent it, as one of the many loving letters that the woman would write in the course of the years, preoccupied as she was with her loved ones' health.

The two had been apart for months and couldn't wait for Cosimo's return to finally get married.

". . . And I would like to be able to send you a warm cape so that you wouldn't feel cold. I hope that the cockcrow's illness is not bothering you and Lorenzo too much. I only await the day when I will be able to see you again." The cockcrow's illness was an expression used for gout, an illness that the Medici family suffered from. The shooting pain to the big toes caused by the illness often manifested in the morning.

Cosimo delicately closed the letter and put it in his pocket, then, observing his travel comrades, he murmured one last sentence before finishing his meal. "After all, sooner or later, all men find a place to go to."

In spite of Baldassarre Cossa's fall from grace, the experience of Constance had been excellent for Cosimo. Despite his young age and relative inexperience, he had the chance to collaborate and brilliantly interact with some of the most prestigious bankers and businessmen of all of Europe, including the very powerful Fugger family.

Work and meetings also allowed Cosimo to expand the already wide list of contacts and acquaintances of the Banco Medici, a circle of public relations that would have provided a noticeable number of business rapports to occur even years after the council.

Once back home, Cosimo and his brother enjoyed a few days of rest before putting themselves back to work seriously.

Not a lot of time elapsed before Piccarda reassured them about the promise they had received months before. "Your father will keep his word. You, Cosimo, will be able to marry Contessina shortly, and the same for you and Ginevra, Lorenzo. I am myself seeing that the weddings proceed in the best possible way," she said.

The Ginevra who was promised to Lorenzo was called Ginevra di Giovanni di Amerigo dei Cavalcanti; she was part of one of the most ancient merchant families of Florence. The Cavalcanti had lost part of their importance toward the end of the fourteenth century, but a union with a prominent member of the Medici would open the doors to public office, so much so that thirteen priors were to be counted in the family from the middle of the fifteenth century until the middle of the next.

"Are you happy about your upcoming marriage, brother?" Cosimo asked Lorenzo.

"Happy and satisfied to be marrying almost at the same time as you, Cosimo," replied Lorenzo. The younger brother's face, framed by long, dark hair, was more relaxed and delicate than Cosimo's, and did not hide any malice. Just like when they were children, then adolescents, the relationship between the two brothers continued to be one of sincere love, devoid of any conflict.

Maybe Lorenzo's meeker and more docile nature, which nevertheless knew how to hold its own when confronted with others or with business matters, had contributed to the harmony of that relationship. The fact is that Lorenzo followed Cosimo, without any envy or jealousy, for better or worse, supporting and facilitating him both in political matters as well as in cultural ones.

Both weddings were happily celebrated in 1416. In the same

year, Contessina gave birth to Cosimo's firstborn, Piero. For some time, husband and wife went to live in the Bardi palace, situated beyond the Arno in an area that in antiquity had been dubbed as "lice ridden" but now was full of palaces belonging to rich families.

Lorenzo and his wife remained to live in his family home, and only later had two sons: Francesco, who died in infancy, and Pierfrancesco, born in 1430, who carried forward that branch of the family.

Cosimo and Lorenzo resumed their work with full power.

Often Cosimo was on the frontline to manage some of the other commercial activities of the family, such as meeting the managers of the woolen mills that belonged to, or were financed by, the Medici.

During those years, Florence possessed at least 180 factories of which neither the kind nor the number of laborers is known for certain, but it can be speculated that they were mainly woolen mills.

What is certain, however, is that during those years competition from other Italian cities was becoming increasingly pressing. Several Florentine trading houses had begun to weave their fabrics outside of Florence, for instance in Milan.

At the same time, the situation had also been made difficult by the birth in other nations, such as England and France, of industries of an increasingly good quality, thus decreasing both the quantity of fabrics produced for export outside of Italy, and the profits related to this trade. Cosimo read the report redacted by the manager of the woolen mill, a small and nervous man who was startled at the slightest sight of the yet placid Cosimo.

"We have lost about a third of the income," said Cosimo. "Tell me, what do you think may be the reason behind that? Fewer orders? A lack of clients?"

"Lack of workers, signor Cosimo," said the sorrowful wool mill manager.

"Lack of workers? Did Florence have a new uprising I was not aware of?" replied Cosimo sarcastically.

Over the years, after the Ciompi Uproar or other turbulent times, some laborers had left Florence to find refuge in nearby cities, leaving several factories inoperative. Every period of inactivity or lack of adequate laborers was a period of scarcity for business, caused by the inferior quality of production.

"The workers we have employed are good, but there is no generational turnover. The new workers are not up to the old ones, and it shows in the inferior quality of our products," replied the manager.

"Can you replace them with other, more skilled people? I'm sure Florence does not lack unemployed workers looking for a stable job and a salary," said Cosimo.

"It's always the same people. It's a never-ending cycle. Even if I replace one, his substitute would be equally mediocre. There is no turnover, as I told you," replied the increasingly sorrowful manager.

"Let's hire some outside workers, then. Not only do we have to maintain the high standards of what we produce, but we need to strive to improve it even more," replied Cosimo. "And by employing outside workers we could take advantage of their skills."

"Using some new methods, we could even become able to make cheaper products," replied the manager convincingly.

"That's right," replied Cosimo. "But only if we can guarantee the best possible quality—never forget that. And if by using these new methods we will make shoddy products, we had better destroy them."

The manager nodded while taking note of his boss's directives.

"In Florence it is better to destroy goods not up to standards. It would be the stupidest way of ruining a trade," said Cosimo, realizing after a moment that he had quoted his father's exact same words when he brought him, Lorenzo, and their mother to visit the headquarters of the Arte della Lana many years before.

"Is that all, signor Cosimo?" asked the manager.

Cosimo nodded, and after saying goodbye to the man, he headed toward the exit and opened the door. Cosimo stopped for a few moments on the threshold, staring at the road full of citizens busy with their day: common citizens, *petite bourgeoisie*, and wealthy people, all types that Cosimo knew well, but who possessed something different. Suddenly, Cosimo had an intuition, and before the manager had the time to ask him if he had forgotten anything, he turned again to the man. He had to tell him immediately about the thought he just had. Rather, he wanted him to see it with his own eyes.

"Follow me to the door. I want to show you something that, if adequately used, will improve our business even more."

"But, signor Cosimo, I'm very busy right now. There's the outside workers matter to sort out and . . ." replied the manager hesitatingly.

"It won't take more than a minute if you stop mumbling and join me," replied Cosimo, delicately taking the man by his arm. Cosimo brought him to the door's threshold, showing him the road with an ample gesture of the hand.

"Can you see it?" he said.

The manager kept his eyes wide open to try to understand where and what to look at. "Well, signor Cosimo, I reckon I can see some, uh, I, well . . ."

Cosimo put a hand on his shoulder and pointed to some pedestrians. Clothing fashion had changed, and in Florence, like in other cities, men and women, especially those belonging to the upper classes, but also people who wanted to flaunt a bit of luxury, had started to wear silk and brocade rather than wool.

"We shall start to differentiate production and open shops specialized in selling silk," said Cosimo.

"Wouldn't that be a risk?" asked the manager. "Our citizens might soon get tired of it and go back to their old tastes."

"There will always be demand for high-quality goods, and that is something we Florentines know how to do very well. Am I wrong?" replied Cosimo.

"No, but it could happen that . . ." the manager tried to continue.

"Do as I say and stop worrying," concluded Cosimo. "We are the principal backers of your mill and it is in our interest too that business will always thrive."

In spite of the profits obtained from the strong internal consumption and, as Cosimo liked to say, from the great need for luxury of many Florentine people, the silk industry never compensated completely for the losses suffered from the wool business, nor did it ever replace it in terms of importance.

The Florentine state, seized by the same intuitions as Cosimo, in an attempt to favor the industry of local silk production, decreed a prohibition to halt the excessive emigration of laborers because of the risk of them creating industries outside of the Florentine territory.

Indeed, according to the decree, "Since in Florence the

golden brocades and silken fabrics are manufactured in a more perfect way than the rest of the whole world, it is prohibited to any Florentine to manufacture or commission the manufacturing of brocades or silken fabrics, or to establish a company with this purpose, in places which are not in Florence," with the threat of the death penalty and confiscation of all resources for the transgressors.

But the years that immediately followed the council brought even bigger changes for Cosimo, his family, and the whole of Florence. First, from May 1417 to January 1418, Florentine citizens fell victim to a new wave of the plague, less than six years after the previous epidemic, which had resulted in a high mortality rate and the escape of many people to neighboring cities in search of shelter. This time, the plague wave was much shorter in duration. In those months the city was able to better face the epidemic than in the past, thanks to the unexpected cohesion of its richer and more powerful citizens. These men, headed by Giovanni di Bicci, in spite of belonging to different political factions, closed ranks by helping the citizens with financial donations and by building structures where sick people could be cared for or even recover.

But in spite of these efforts, the plague claimed an illustrious victim: the old Maso degli Albizzi. Maso was already in his eighties at that time, and the chronicles differ on the matter of his death; it may have been caused by the plague or simply the effects of aging.

The death of Maso, with the subsequent handover of power to his son Rinaldo, influenced the weight balance of power in Florence. Less gifted than Cosimo, and less charismatic than Maso, Rinaldo had an impulsive nature, audacity, and stubbornness, and he aspired to concentrate his father's power even further, aiming to make Florence his own personal dominion.

Moreover, Rinaldo saw the death of his father as an occasion to placate his ancient envy toward Cosimo and finally get rid of him and the Medici family. The restlessness of the new lord of Florence, backed by allies who were both younger and less reflective than those on whom his father could count, continued to be arduously appeased by the counsel of Niccolò da Uzzano.

But Rinaldo underestimated the way a group of more moderate oligarchs gathered around the figure of the old Niccolò. Far removed from Rinaldo's extremist tendencies, Niccolò wanted, of course, to prevent an overthrow of the oligarchy, but also for Florence to fall under the dominion of a sole man.

On top of the fear that Cosimo and Rinaldo could become despots, Niccolò worried more than anything that because of the deep benevolence that was bestowed upon them by the people, the ones likely to overthrow the oligarchy would be precisely Cosimo and Giovanni.

In 1417, during a visit to a thermal bath far away from the city in order to alleviate the symptoms of the gout that afflicted them, Cosimo and Lorenzo discussed new assignments with Giovanni. The three men were finally able to relax after turbulent months, and the conversations had changed course to loftier subjects than work and politics.

"I've received a letter from Bracciolini," said Cosimo. "He decided to go back to the St. Gallen's monastery and keep searching there, where he recently found the complete manuscript of Quintilian's *Institutiones Oratoriae*."

"Do you reckon fate will assist him once more?" asked Lorenzo.

"Yes, I believe it will. In his letter he also enthusiastically mentions the discovery of new orations by Cicero and some treatises by Vitruvius and Valerius Flaccus."

"I heard that he has been accompanied in his research by Bartolomeo Aragazzi da Montepulciano and Cencio de' Rustici. Good, brilliant men," said Giovanni.

"I know you wouldn't want to be anywhere else in the world, brother," said Lorenzo in a playful tone.

"I wouldn't mind it," replied Cosimo. "If only I didn't have to help Contessina raise our little Piero, not mentioning all the new commitments."

"When are you planning to have a second son, brother?" asked Lorenzo.

"Soon, I hope. Contessina and I would like to have more than two," replied Cosimo. "But one thing at a time."

"What about you, Lorenzo? When will you give a grandchild to me and your mother?" asked Giovanni.

"One thing at a time, Father, like Cosimo just said," replied an amused Lorenzo.

"As long as we won't have to wait too long. Piccarda and I are not that young anymore, and before dying we would love to see you with an heir, like Cosimo," replied Giovanni. "For instance, I remember that when I married your mother, our respective parents insisted for us to . . ."

A servant brought some cloths and a bucket of fresh water to allow the three men to refresh their faces.

"Ah, good boy! And don't forget to bring us more cloths and water in a short while!" said Giovanni, interrupting his previous argument midway.

Father and sons gave themselves a few moments of silence, slowly breathing the healing vapors of the thermal waters; even though the effect on their gout was relatively limited, those vapors managed to relax their bodies and spirits.

Giovanni broke that silence for a matter much more important than the anecdote he was digging up again. "We really should be worried about Maso's death, you know."

Neither Lorenzo nor Cosimo lost much of their composure. They hadn't lived under the oligarchic regime as long as Giovanni had, but during their lives they had already seen and heard enough to get used to the constant tension of the city.

"It was inevitable that power would remain in the hands of the Albizzi, Father. There were no conditions that would have allowed things to change," replied Lorenzo, with the wet cloth still draped on his face.

"I'm aware of that, Lorenzo. I would be naive or infinitely stupid to think that the oligarchs would have let power slip from their hands after Maso's death. But then again, there are Albizzi and Albizzi and it would be preferable if the oligarchy were to be represented by people such as Niccolò da Uzzano or Gino Capponi," continued Giovanni. "That's why a man like Maso will always be preferable to a man like Rinaldo."

Giovanni looked at his son Cosimo, as he also still had the wet cloth on his face.

"You should be especially worried about that, Cosimo, since you know only too well the feelings Rinaldo has toward you," added Giovanni. "And don't be fooled into thinking that his father's death or his new responsibilities have made him a wiser man."

"Well, I'm not a fool, Father. I know Rinaldo very well and I'm aware of the sentiments he has—and always had—toward me. And, above all, I've never forgotten your speech about envy," replied Cosimo, now removing the warm cloth from his face. "In fact, I have treasured it."

"What do you think might happen, Father?" asked Lorenzo.

"All or nothing, Lorenzo," replied Giovanni. "They may leave us alone as they have done so far, or decide on some more or less restrictive measures. It will depend on how big a threat they consider us to be."

"If anything should happen, Father, our family will not be caught unaware," added Lorenzo.

"But we must always try to be careful," replied Giovanni. "Remember that the city's oligarchs never looked at us with particular fondness, since Salvestro's role during the Ciompi Uproar."

"But you're forgetting," intervened Cosimo, "that you've also told us about Uncle Vieri's role when another tumult exploded a few years later. When the poor in the city asked him to guide them against the rich and powerful, he spoke to the Signoria and managed to have the peaceful dispersal of the rebels and not be punished by the Signoria for having been asked to lead the revolt."

"What are you trying to point out?" asked Lorenzo.

"That our relationship with the oligarchs has always been a fractured one, for better or for worse," replied Cosimo. "But, if and when the moment comes, we should answer back with the same shrewdness—although different in their forms—displayed by both Vieri and Salvestro."

The power handover from Maso to Rinaldo wasn't the only event to discuss; another pressing situation had arisen. It involved Baldassarre Cossa, the ex-pope, who was still incarcerated in the castle of Heidelberg after being deposed during the Council of Constance.

"The bail money for Cossa's liberation has been fixed to more than thirty thousand florins," commented Giovanni.

His two sons remained silent for a moment. Maybe after the exhausting trip to Germany and miraculously avoiding being imprisoned like Cossa—or worse—Cosimo and Lorenzo did not want to dwell on this matter, at least for now.

"To pay more than thirty thousand florins to free a former pope who has been deposed, imprisoned, and is probably without any property or wealth left?" questioned Lorenzo, breaking the silence.

The slightly cynical skepticism of Cosimo's brother had several justifications, because to still count on Cossa's friendship would be an entirely lost bet, if not a dangerous one. Giovanni turned to Cosimo: "Do you have anything to add, my son? Do you share your brother's opinion on this matter?"

Cosimo pondered what he was about to say and then expressed himself in favor of his brother. "Lorenzo may be right, Father. Besides, you know only too well that our Roman branch has often lent more money that it gained." Cosimo was partly right, because the high positions of the Roman church often spent enormous sums of money, pushing their accounts into overdrafts of considerable sums.

"I must admit that it's partly true, but you're forgetting that, despite what you've just said, the investments made through the Roman branch have always given us a considerable income," replied Giovanni, before making another observation. "And you're forgetting that at least half of our annual profits comes from that branch."

"With all due respect, Father, we are talking about a man who during his youth made his fortune with piracy. The sins from his past have come back to punish him in his old age. What he could have offered or promised us in his old office has now entirely vanished," added Lorenzo, this time more clear-headed in outlining his skepticism toward Cossa, who, after all, during the years in which he had "served" in the Church had demonstrated a religious calling equal to zero.

"Don't you reckon we also have the duty to preserve our family's name in this matter?" replied Giovanni. "What would they think of me—of us—if we now abandon a man who has fallen from grace and whom I have served for years with my bank and whom I called, in the letters we exchanged, 'dearest friend'?"

As promised, the servant returned with more cloths and a new bucket of fresh water. With a wave of his hand, Cosimo made him understand that it wasn't the right moment to disturb the two bickerers.

"So that's the way it is, Father. It is just a matter of preserving our personal prestige," pressed Lorenzo. "That's the reason you're willing to give an unfair chance to a man who no longer has any value? I know how important it is for you to do what you consider the right thing, but this feels to me the reasoning of an overly sentimental man."

"It's not merely a matter of personal prestige, the good name of the bank and our family is at stake!" answered Giovanni.

While the conflict between father and son was starting to degenerate, Cosimo was thinking in silence. Lorenzo expressed his arguments to Giovanni in an increasingly direct manner. "I haven't said anything when our mother thought that even someone like Cossa would redeem himself and be touched by divine light, but I'd have never thought that even you . . ."

"What your mother thought in good faith could also be my

same reasoning," answered Giovanni. "Therefore I ask you to stop talking like that and . . ."

Cosimo suddenly raised his head, interrupting the quarrel.

"No more," said Cosimo. "It is neither the time nor the place. But, above all, the argument is not worthy of us." Giovanni and Lorenzo stopped immediately, embarrassed for losing their proverbial family temper and for starting to fight.

"Lorenzo, it is true that your point of view is partially correct, and I do share it partly as well," continued Cosimo. "But I must admit that our father is right." Neither Lorenzo nor Giovanni intervened while listening to Cosimo.

"If we play our cards right, not only will we continue to preserve our reputation as a family and a business, but we will make enormous gains," continued Cosimo. "Are you ready to listen to what I'm about to say?"

Giovanni and Lorenzo nodded, and that day of relaxation at the thermal baths was soon transformed into another brilliant intuition of the Medici, an intuition that would allow them to prosper even more in the coming years.

Chapter Five

QUOD SCRIPSI, SCRIPSI

In 1418, Cosimo, who was now twenty-nine, paid the enormous bail for Cossa who was able to enjoy freedom again after four years of imprisonment, and after considering the possibility of running away once more, maybe even abroad, Cossa reasoned that he was too ill and tired by the trials of the previous years to risk being newly imprisoned or condemned to die burning at the stake.

It was thus that the aged adventurer accepted the invitation from Giovanni and his sons to move into a villa in Florence that had been made available to him, where he would be cared for, and waited on hand and foot, just like when he was still pope.

"Welcome, Your Eminence."

"Have a good day, Your Holiness."

"Enjoy your meal, Your Excellency."

The courtesies and efforts of the servants put at Cossa's disposal were almost exaggerated, but the man liked it.

Cosimo was doing even better; the brilliancy of his plan had especially surprised his father. His son's new intuition had given Giovanni further confirmation that Cosimo would be his worthy successor. One evening while they sat at the dinner table together, Giovanni brought up the subject with his sons.

"Our already solid business will be considered even more reputable. Who, in Italy or in Europe, would think that we would have used such an enormous amount of money if our safes were not bursting with profits?" said a very pleased Giovanni.

"And your—or rather, our—loyalty to Baldassarre will remain unchanged. And thus, not one of our adversaries will claim that we have forsaken a disgraced man," replied Cosimo.

"And we're giving hospitality to a man who, despite all his peculiarities, has guided a part of Christianity," added Giovanni.

"Our prestige will grow even bigger, both on a social and business level," replied Cosimo with satisfaction.

"And thus, in a short amount of time, we will manage to get back what we spent," added Giovanni.

"I knew you would be satisfied, Father," said Cosimo.

"More than satisfied," said Giovanni. "But right now there's another matter that requires your shrewdness."

"I think I understand what you're about to say," replied Cosimo.

"Yes. We must continue being papal bankers. We must convince Pope Martin we are worthy of his trust," said Giovanni.

"That will be a harder task. Martin is a member of the Colonna family, as you know," replied Cosimo. "One of the oldest and most prestigious patrician families in Rome. Such important men could be stubborn and unwilling to change their ideas."

"Not for any want in our activity, of course," said Giovanni, huffing with frustration. "But it will be hard for him to swallow the fact that we have liberated the man deposed by the council who elected him pope."

"We will come up with a solution for this problem as well, Father. And perhaps, once again, good fortune will keep an eye on us," concluded Cosimo.

Good fortune really helped the Medici. Indeed, from the end of the events of Constance, Martin V hadn't gone back to Rome yet, where the situation had become rather turbulent after the council. During his long wandering through Italy, Pope Martin V reached Florence in 1419, establishing himself in the convent of Santa Maria Novella. From that moment they called him "the Florentine Lateran," because the place had become a papal residence.

That visit provided Florence and its citizens with even more prestige, in spite of the oligarchs' nervousness, who only that year had instigated general apprehension with a new provision regarding the persecution of the confraternities.

Almost all born during the previous century, the confraternities were associations that had a great number of affiliates, and carried out charitable and beneficial work. Fearing that behind their disinterested services toward Florence could be hiding conspirators with the intention to overthrow the regime, the oligarchs closed off their premises and confiscated their registries and estates.

These associations came back by changing their name into companies, but later they were again cyclically persecuted and prohibited, especially in other delicate periods for the oligarchic regime. In the meantime, Cosimo continued with his plan, determined to exploit the opportunity obtained through fate with Martin's stay in Florence.

Without losing precious time, Cosimo convinced Cossa and Martin to reconcile publicly. For Cossa it meant being able to live his last days in peace, while for Martin it indicated a new proof of power that demonstrated even more that he had become the first pope to reign without rivals, after decades of conflicts in the Church.

Martin accepted willingly the reconciliation with Cossa, even granting him an honorary title. The pope tried to do the same with Giovanni, offering him the title of count. But Giovanni refused, not wanting to elevate himself above the other citizens by becoming an aristocrat—or, according to the malicious tongues of the enemies of the family, "in order to continue being among the people and keep doing business at its best."

Cossa died that same year, 1419, but not before appointing Cosimo and Giovanni the executors of his will. In exchange, many years since their first meeting, Giovanni paid homage to him by having a beautiful tomb built in the Florence Baptistery by Donatello and Michelozzo.

The plan to become the new pontiff's bankers did not go equally well, because Martin, not entirely trusting the Medici, preferred to assign the management of the pontifical finances to the Spini family. This left Cosimo with a bitter taste, but even more so for Giovanni, who worried about the relationships with the Spini, his mother's family of origin, since these had been broken off years before.

Pope Martin was still in Florence, and during the last months of preparations before his definitive return to Rome in 1420, one day he found himself visiting the Florence Baptistery together with Cosimo and Giovanni. The three men were slowly walking inside the building, while Martin lingered around that architectural marvel and the many pieces of art contained in it. Even though both he and Giovanni were sorry for Cosimo's failed plan, they maintained their usual impeccable behavior with the pontiff.

". . . And I hope you didn't take too badly the refused concession to administer the papal finances," said Martin.

"Absolutely not, Your Holiness," replied Giovanni, putting on a brave face. "The word of the pope is law, and we Medici have always respected the law."

"More than right. We'll have the chance to discuss this matter again in the future, if my relationship with the Spini family should come to an end. But now let us talk about less earthly and more pleasant matters for the spirit," said Martin while observing the mosaics of the internal dome of the baptistery. "Tell me, is it true that it took almost one hundred years to complete all the mosaics?"

"At least one hundred years, Your Holiness," replied Cosimo. "Incredibly long and expensive works, made by Venetian mosaicists using preliminary drawings by great Florentine painters such as Cimabue or Coppo di Marcovaldo. The works for mosaics have also been supervised by the Arte di Calimala, our oldest guild that I am sure you've heard about."

"Of course I have. Who doesn't know the Florentine guilds and their successes in financial and commercial endeavors?" replied Martin with sincere admiration.

The pope pointed at a zone in the baptistery where work was still underway. "What about that one?" asked Martin. "Is that perhaps the new bronze door I've heard so much about?"

"That is correct, Your Holiness. The north door," replied

Cosimo. "But it will need more time to be completed. At least two or three more years, I should imagine." Cosimo's estimate was correct. Although the artisans began work in 1403, the door would not be finished until 1424.

"I cannot wait to see it. Yet, it is worth waiting days, months, and even years to be able to admire such wonders. What sacred histories have been chosen to appear in the mosaics? Who is the artist? How and when was he selected for the job?" asked Martin impatiently.

"You'd better not ask any of these questions to the workers—they're a surly lot. I hope, however, that your curiosity will be fulfilled as soon as possible," replied Cosimo with a joke. "Allow us, though, to preserve some mystery on the scenes that will appear in the mosaics. We don't want to give anything away just yet. As for your other questions, I'm sure my father will be able to answer all of them better than I could ever do."

A big and bearded middle-aged laborer passed through, running between the three men while carrying a half-open bag full of provisions, amongst which was a large piece of meat.

"Out of the way, excellent signori. Out of the way, Your Eminence," grumbled the laborer while trying not to hit any of the bystanders with the heavy bag.

The man was going toward the outside of the baptistery, in an area restricted to laborers, where shortly he would use that meat to prepare the *peposo*, a flavorsome red wine stew said to have been the favorite work dish of Florentine architects and laborers.

Martin observed with curiosity the man's walk toward the exit: He was so ungainly in both his body shape and demeanor, yet he was working to make even more beautiful what was already one of the most beautiful buildings that the pope had ever admired in his life.

Then the pope turned to Giovanni, intrigued by Cosimo's words. "Are you really better prepared on this subject than your son Cosimo, Giovanni?"

"I believe so, Your Holiness. But it's merely a matter of old age, and not of a brighter acumen," replied Giovanni. "And also because I had the chance to sit in the committee that decided to employ the artist Lorenzo Ghiberti to work on the north door of the baptistery. It was around 1401 or 1402—so many years have passed since then."

"Is that so? That's quite admirable, Giovanni, and a further confirmation that you are indeed a man fond of art and culture. I think Florence really owes you a lot on account of both," replied Martin. "What about you, Cosimo, do you remember what happened at the time?"

"What I remember most is the pride my brother and I felt for our father," replied Cosimo. "I also remember something about a dispute over whether to give the final commission to Lorenzo Ghiberti or Filippo Brunelleschi."

"Ah, yes, I do remember something now," replied Martin. "Some friends who happened to travel through Florence at that time told me that part of the committee supported Ghiberti, while another part pushed for Brunelleschi's victory."

"And I was amongst those who thought they were both equally worthy of the task, Your Holiness," continued Giovanni. "In the end, to settle the competition once and for all, we gave them one year to sculpt a small bronze tile on the theme of Isaac's sacrifice."

"Marvelous!" exclaimed Martin. "Have you had the chance to be involved in other similar committees?"

"Yes, at times. However, I hope to leave my sons to deal with this sort of matter soon," replied Giovanni, putting a hand on Cosimo's shoulder.

The aroma of meat, which had been marinated in red wine together with pepper and aromatic herbs and put in the oven used by the laborers to cook, started to spread inside the baptistery. That heavenly smell did not distract the three men from their conversation on art and patronage.

"Recently, I had the chance to take care of a very important matter," added Giovanni with a hint of pride. "I was put in change of a committee to commission the construction of a hospital for orphaned children. It will be called *Ospedale degli Innocenti*, Hospital of the Innocents, and Filippo Brunelleschi will be its leading architect."

"A very commendable endeavor that denotes true Christian charity," replied Martin, who continued to wander around the baptistery, which he had by now carefully covered and studied from top to bottom. There was only one part he hadn't yet seen, related to a question to which he had dedicated part of his stay in Florence.

"But tell me, has Cossa's tomb been completed? And who worked on it?" asked Martin.

"Donatello and Michelozzo, but it hasn't been completed yet," replied Giovanni.

"I would like to see it in order to conclude this visit to the baptistery. I doubt I will be able to see it before departing to Rome, and I don't know when I'll be back in Florence," said Martin.

Giovanni and Cosimo took Martin in front of the funeral monument, which in spite of not being completed already displayed magnificence. The pope was immediately fascinated by that beautiful work, built with marble and golden bronze, and situated between two columns on the right of the main altar.

Martin paused to look at the beauty of the sculpted coffin on the actual tomb, and he couldn't help making a small joke, at the same time celebrating Donatello and Michelozzo's ability.

"Splendid, absolutely magnificent. I can only imagine how it will look when it will be finished. It is certainly true what people say," said Martin to the two men. "The best-looking papal tombs are the ones sculpted by your Florentine artists."

Martin corrected that statement with a small laugh. "Papal and *antipapal* tombs, I mean. And let's hope I won't need one for myself anytime soon." Then the pope decided to give a further look at the monument and lingered on the Latin incision Giovanni and Cosimo had decided to have affixed on the tomb: *Joannes quodam Papa XXIII*—John XXIII was pope.

In a second Martin's mood changed from day to night. "This is an insult to the pope and to the Catholic Church, Giovanni! That incision claims that Cossa was still pope at the time of his death! It's a sacrilege toward all men of faith!" Martin exclaimed, now suddenly furious.

Before Giovanni could reply, taken by surprise by that sudden attack, Cosimo interposed himself between his father and Martin. "That is no insult, Your Holiness," said Cosimo.

"No insult? And how would you justify that incision, then, to me and to all Catholics, Cosimo?" pressed Martin.

"I don't want to justify anything, Your Holiness. That incision was not intended as a sin or done with a sinful mind. Simply, *quod scripsi, scripsi*. What I have written, I have written," replied Cosimo with great coldness.

"You should remember, then, that what has been said, has been said," said Martin. "There are now two things I shall try to accomplish during my papacy—to remove from Rome the Orsini family and to ruin all the Florentines!"

"We shall see who will prevail over time, Your Holiness. I am sorry to say that, but *de secunda non timemus*, we are not afraid of that second thing."

After that episode, which had poisoned that apparently pleasant day, Martin hastened his preparations for departure, hoping to return to Rome as soon as possible—far away from those Medici who had held their own, not just in words but in shrewdness as well.

And almost as a last insult, when the pope left Florence on the ninth of September 1420, the Signoria ordered that nine of the main citizens accompany him to the border of the Republic's territory. One of them was precisely Giovanni di Bicci.

The year 1420 saw a major change inside the Banco Medici. Benedetto passed away that year, leaving Florence's branch without its managing director, and the old Giovanni without his partner with whom he had shared the very beginnings of the company and its successes.

One morning Giovanni summoned Cosimo, Lorenzo, and Ilarione in his office and, once he sat down in his favorite chair, began one of the most important speeches of his life.

"I think you know only too well the reason why I summoned all of you here," started the man. "Ilarione, allow me to begin by saying that your brother was an exceptional man and that I could not have hoped for a better partner throughout all these years."

"Thank you, Giovanni, for your kind words," replied Ilarione. "You must know that my brother thought the same about you. My whole family is indebted to you, because you helped to shape the future of us all."

"The respect we had for each other was mutual and he did many important deeds for my family's future too. The success of the Banco Medici is largely due to his incessant work. It has come time, however, to appoint a new general manager," continued Giovanni. "You have been a very valuable associate to us, both in Rome and here in Florence. My sons have been witnesses of the work you have done for us during your journey to Constance."

"It's true, Ilarione," Lorenzo chimed in. "You've always worked in an impeccable manner, and not only in Germany."

"Absolutely. It was thanks to your work that our journey was so carefully recorded," Cosimo echoed.

"Very well," said Giovanni. "Since I don't see any objections, it is decided that Ilarione shall be appointed as the new general manager of the Medici bank. I have already decided the name of the new local manager, but we shall discuss that later. In the meantime . . ."

Giovanni opened the drawer and took out a contract, signaling Ilarione to come closer to the desk to read it.

"Come closer too, my sons," he added, gesturing to Cosimo and Lorenzo. "There's something I want you to read."

Ilarione read the contract first and, having reached the point where Giovanni wanted his sons to read it as well, he looked the man in the eyes and said while nodding, "I agree with your decision, Giovanni."

The document reached Lorenzo's hands; he nodded as well. "I, too, agree with it, Father." It was finally Cosimo's turn. He slowly re-read several times that specific point in the contract, incredulous at what he saw.

Almost hesitant, quite a rare occurrence for him, he asked his father, "The contract is between Ilarione, Lorenzo, and myself. Your name is not in it. Does this mean that . . . ?"

"Yes, Cosimo, you're correct," replied Giovanni. "I am sixty and in the last few years I have seen many times that you and your brother are more than ready to take my place. And you especially, my son. I knew you were ready when I saw you hold your own against Pope Martin. I could not hope to leave the *banco* in better hands than yours."

"But you've always considered the bank as the most important part of your life, Father," said Lorenzo. "How will you ever manage to stop working for it?"

"Oh, but it's not true that I won't work for it anymore," replied Giovanni with a laugh. "I've decided to remain on in a counseling role. If you don't mind, of course!"

"That's obviously fine with us, Father. It is decided, then, that Banco Medici will change its managers, and may it enjoy the same success it's had so far," replied Cosimo.

Giovanni took a pitcher of wine, which he kept hidden in the deep drawer of a nearby cabinet, and four cups. "This wine has been produced in our vineyards. This one is special—I've prepared and sweetened it myself using herbs and berries," said Giovanni. "I've preserved it carefully for an occasion such as this one."

Giovanni poured the wine, and the four men raised their cups.

"May the Banco Medici retain all its success," reaffirmed Cosimo.

"No, Cosimo," Giovanni corrected him. "May the Banco Medici enjoy an even greater success and become known throughout the whole world."

~

After this news, Cosimo, Lorenzo, and Ilarione went back to work, agreeing that now more than ever they must stay in constant contact with each other in order to carry out a general reorganization of the Medici Bank.

"It is decided that this year's capital will be of twenty-four thousand florins. Lorenzo and I will put in eight thousand florins each and you, Ilarione, will need to invest an equal sum," proclaimed Cosimo the following day at his desk. "Do you all agree with this plan?"

"Yes, we do," they both replied.

"We shall discuss in future the line to be adopted should minority partners decide to invest in order to expand the capital. Profits will be shared equally on the proportion of the money invested initially," continued Cosimo. "Do you also agree on this account?"

"Yes," Lorenzo and Ilarione agreed once more.

"How shall we divide the capital?" asked Lorenzo.

"Six thousand florins to the Roman branch, seven thousand and five hundred to the Venetian one, and the rest will stay in Florence," answered Cosimo.

"There are other matters to discuss," intervened Ilarione.

"Very well," replied Cosimo. "I was just getting to that. There are three main points. First of all, we must terminate our partnerships with textile mills and businesses with which we are losing money."

"I see. There's a woolen mill that's been in losing money for months now," replied Ilarione while jotting down with Lorenzo the points that Cosimo had discussed.

"Good. Second point—all the contracts stipulated under

your brother's management are to be considered expired from the moment of his death," continued Cosimo. "Before signing any of them again, we shall evaluate each, one by one, and decide which are worthy of being reprised."

"Are you referring to commercial contracts or to those about people employed in our branches?" asked Ilarione.

"Both of them," anticipated Lorenzo.

"Exactly. Excellent, dear brother," replied Cosimo.

"And what would the third point be?" asked Lorenzo.

"It is to regain access to the Roman curia as papal bankers," replied Cosimo.

"Even after what happened with Pope Martin?" asked Cosimo's brother.

"Ah!" Ilarione erupted with laughter. "I wish I could have been there to see that fight! I can only imagine how funny it must have been to see you and old Giovanni arguing with the pope!"

"It wasn't particularly amusing, Ilarione, that I can assure you. But I will make sure you are there should it happen again," replied Cosimo. "And you, Lorenzo, we cannot change what happened with Martin, but nothing is forever. Not the Medici, not the Spini, not even the pope. Things are going to change, sooner or later, and we'll have to push them once again in our favor."

Cosimo was right on this last prediction. Some time after, a new piece of happy news concerned him personally. The following year, to the delight of Contessina and Cosimo, they had a second child, a boy they named Giovanni.

More tired but always active, the elder Giovanni di Bicci journeyed to visit them in their home, both to meet his newborn grandson and to communicate some major news to Cosimo. His son and daughter-in-law were waiting for him in the living room, with Cosimo holding the newborn in his arms.

"Such a beautiful baby. He looks exactly like you," said Contessina to her husband.

"You're the beautiful one, my beloved wife. He looks like you," replied Cosimo. Piero, who was five years old, came closer to his parents with wide-open arms.

"I want to hold my little brother!" he said with the singsong voice of a young child.

"Only if you prove yourself to be reliable and careful, Piero," replied Contessina. "Your brother Giovanni is not a toy. He's a fragile little thing who needs a lot of attention."

A few tears rolled down Piero's disappointed face; in order to beg forgiveness Cosimo gave Giovanni to Contessina and readily took his firstborn in his arms. After making him spin in the air a few times the boy's tears transformed into laughter.

"You listen to your mother, Piero. You can watch over your brother when you are older and more responsible, just like every bigger brother in the world. But for now, keep laughing!"

One of Cosimo and Contessina's servants went to open the door, allowing Giovanni and his personal servant to enter.

"Giovanni, how good to see you on such a blessed day," Contessina welcomed him. "But why are you practically alone? You could have come over at least with a little escort."

"Thank you, but I do not need it," replied Giovanni. "I'm not one of those men who is too wealthy or too self-important to go around with an escort just to show my social status."

"I didn't mean to offend you, Giovanni. I was just worried that someone could have hurt or robbed you," Contessina tried to explain.

"Oh, I know that. I know you have only said that because you have my well-being in mind," replied Giovanni, showing a hint of a smile. "It's just something so many people ask me about. When I was younger it was taken for granted that a rich man could walk freely around without an escort."

Contessina gently nodded while Giovanni continued his point of view in a melancholic way. "But perhaps it's just the blurred memory of a man who's becoming older by the day. When you reach my age, the past always seems better than it actually was."

"Many citizens ask me the same thing they ask you, Father," observed Cosimo, trying not to make his father feel too sad about his past youth.

"It's the common fate of those who are successful in life," replied Giovanni. "The divine penance for those who would prefer to live their lives in a modest way but are forced to show to everyone who they have become."

"Stop thinking about that now, Father, and enjoy yourself a little," said Cosimo.

"Come and see your new grandson," said Contessina. "Come and see what a handsome little man he is."

"And there's also your other grandson waiting to play with you, if you're not too tired," added Cosimo.

"I reckon I can still withstand the exuberance of a child that age . . . or at least have a priest at hand in case he makes me too tired and I need to draft my will," joked Giovanni with his typically macabre sense of humor.

Giovanni spent a few happy hours with his two grandchildren;

Cosimo and Contessina were pleased that in spite of having renounced official work at the bank, he would not let the health problems of old age stop him. Rather, he was keeping himself even too busy.

That same evening, while Contessina was putting her sons to bed, Giovanni told Cosimo how the idea of not being closely involved with social matters was nearly impossible to imagine.

"They proposed you become the new *gonfaloniere*, Father?" asked Cosimo to that unexpected piece of news that his father take this prominent post in the city.

"Yes, and I will certainly be elected. But I was not looking for it and both Niccolò da Uzzano and Rinaldo opposed it," replied Giovanni.

"I can imagine the reasons behind Rinaldo's opposition, but why Niccolò? I know he fears us, but I would have expected another kind of opposition from a man like him," said Cosimo.

"It's just as I told you and your brother some time ago. Niccolò believes I would act like Salvestro during the tumult of the Ciompi. He thinks I would support the people during a potential revolt, or even start one myself. I know too well that he believes I've become so wealthy and so popular amongst the citizens just to be elected *gonfaloniere*," replied Giovanni.

"What will you do now?" asked Cosimo.

"I will obviously talk to Niccolò in order to make him change his mind," replied Giovanni.

"And what will you tell him?" asked Cosimo.

"I will tell him the opposite of the sad thoughts I just told Contessina a few moments ago. I will tell him that it's not good to be anchored to what happened in the past, but to think about what will happen in the future," replied Giovanni.

"You'll be a good *gonfaloniere*, Father," added Cosimo.

"Thank you, my son."

That wish from Cosimo was the closest thing to what would have been reality, but a few more years would elapse before the law for which Giovanni would be remembered by the people of Florence would take place. Until then, the following years continued to be full of work for Cosimo. In 1422 he took on the role of consul in Pisa, and in 1424 he found himself working as an agent of the bank branch of Rome and Tivoli.

It was precisely in Rome, where he had gone with Ilarione, that Cosimo managed to finally fulfill one of the last achievements Giovanni had longed for before officially abandoning the bank. Thanks to his contacts and his innate diplomatic skills, Cosimo obtained a meeting with Pope Martin to resume the discussion that had been abruptly cut short a few years before.

On the day of the meeting Cosimo was prepared, and hoped he could strike just the right tone. "Your Holiness, it is a privilege to see you again," he said as he entered the pope's studio, and bowed before him. To avoid unnerving the pontiff too much, Ilarione waited outside for the outcome of this meeting.

Without replying, Martin imperceptibly signaled his bodyguards to leave the room, and then indicated to Cosimo to sit. Now finally set up in Rome and fully aware of the power he had acquired, the pope ostentatiously displayed power and confidence in even the slightest glances, gestures, or words, but Cosimo was not intimidated.

"I expected that you would ask for an appointment first and then send one of your administrators," said the pope coldly.

"In that case I would have asked one of the administrators to request the appointment directly, Your Holiness. Besides, one of my most trusted men is right outside, if you're so willing to meet him," readily replied Cosimo.

"Cosimo de' Medici," said the pope with a mocking smile. "I haven't seen you or your father again since my last stay in Florence, and you're well aware of what happened during that occasion. If I have accepted your request for a meeting despite those . . . past unpleasantries, it's mostly because I want to ask you two questions."

"I am only too glad to answer, Your Holiness. Ask me," responded Cosimo.

"It's your duty to answer to what the head of the Church asks you," replied the pope. "Tell me, Cosimo, is it perhaps that you have requested this appointment because you have heard that the Spini family has gone bankrupt and thus cannot look after the papal finances anymore?"

"Well, we have heard the news in Florence and we are aware you no longer have a papal bank," replied Cosimo. "So, if you're looking for some advice or information concerning the biggest Italian or European banks in order to decide who to contact . . ."

Martin burst into laughter from that implausible reply. "Cosimo, you're one of a kind! You are well aware that I would have never accepted to meet you if I didn't have the need to use your services, and yet you want me to say it out loud! Have you either become too arrogant or confident?"

Cosimo smiled too. "Neither arrogance nor excessive confidence. Rather the opposite, actually. If I asked you myself, I would feel as though I was forcing you, and that would risk ruining my chances. Don't you agree?"

Martin continued to laugh, amused by that affirmation so imbued by the logic of the Medici. "Your reasoning is faultless, Cosimo," said Martin. "That's what I've always liked about you and your family—when you think about business, you always take into consideration even the smallest details."

"This I can't deny, Your Holiness. The smallest details are often more important for the success of a transaction than the transaction itself," replied Cosimo.

"Call in your administrator and we shall talk about the details. The Medici Bank will administer the papal finances again, this I have decided," said Martin.

Cosimo was about to get out, but there was something that the pope hadn't told him yet and he couldn't refrain from asking. "Your Holiness . . ." Cosimo suddenly asked, stopping midway through the door.

"What is it? I've already told you that we shall discuss the details of this new deal along with your administrator," replied the pope.

"What was the second question you wanted to ask me?"

"Ah, Cosimo, Cosimo . . . seeing what we just discussed, I was hoping you forgot about that."

"Ask me what you want. Besides, to answer, as you say . . ." said Cosimo, "it's simply my duty in front of the head of the Church."

"Has Cossa's tomb been completed?" finally asked Martin.

"Yes, it has," replied Cosimo.

"What about the north door of the baptistery?" queried Martin.

"That one too," replied Cosimo.

"Very well, then. We shall meet each other in Florence soon," said Martin. "Now that we settled the unpleasantries of our last meeting and that we are business partners, I want to erase the past and go back to where we left our last conversation."

"Thank you, Your Holiness," replied Cosimo, "for the favor you bestow upon us."

"You should thank me for it," said Martin. "Not everyone

has the chance to see the pope reverse one of his decisions. Remember this, Cosimo. Remember that during the years we will do business together and your bank will become even more powerful and respected."

Upon returning to Florence, Cosimo was eager to meet with Giovanni to tell him he had finally restored the relationship with the curia.

"Only you could have done that, my son," said Giovanni with pride and relief.

"It was only possible thanks to the prestige that you brought to the bank in all these years," replied Cosimo.

"Please, don't be modest with me, as if you didn't work for the bank since you were a young boy," replied Giovanni. "You were very much aware that the situation with the pope was compromised, and I was skeptical myself that we would have been able to save anything from it. But, instead, the outcome is much better than I could have ever hoped for!"

"And it will continue to improve. Ilarione has already met with the pope, along with the general manager of our Roman branch. The secret book has been updated with the first special deposits," added Cosimo. He referred to the secret accounts of the most prominent members of the curia, a procedure used by all of the banks that worked with cardinals, prelates, and other religious figures so that they could contravene, thanks to a bureaucratic loophole, the prohibition on usury proclaimed by the Church.

But meanwhile, the situation in Florence had become more complicated.

Indeed, toward the year 1425, the situation for the dominant oligarchy had worsened, because of the discontent caused by a war against Milan that had been going on for several months, and in which Florence had allied itself with Venice. That war's duration was both long and costly, and at various moments it essentially become a defensive one to protect the city from being conquered by the Milanese troops.

Furthermore, Florentines were antagonized by the lord of the city of Lucca, Paolo Guinigi, a supporter of the Duke of Milan who spent the first weeks of war buying time trying to decide whether to form an alliance with the latter or the closer— and potentially more threatening to Lucca—oligarchs.

The general discontent linked to the war was caused by the very high and numerous taxes that were requested to sustain its costs, and more than once the oligarchs feared that a civil war would erupt once the people found someone to lead them into an uprising. Now both Niccolò da Uzzano and Rinaldo degli Albizzi kept looking with suspicion at the Medici's political immobility. The fear and suspicion that gripped both Niccolò's and Rinaldo's minds for years toward that family, each in a different way, continued to disrupt any chance of restful nights for the two oligarchs.

The war was concluded with a peace treaty signed by the Duke of Milan in 1427, but though the fighting was over, Florence now had the unenviable honor of having to pay more than three million florin, which had been spent to deal with the conflict. Up until that point, taxes in Florence were paid through the system of valuation, which exclusively took into account profits, and hence didn't hit the big landowners. Several rich citizens also managed to pay less than what they actually owned, through stratagems aimed at hiding their true income. As a result, this tax system ended up gouging mainly working class and poor people, who were overtaxed in spite of their meager profits.

On top of the valuation, there were often other taxes that

were established, depending on circumstances. The only solution to collect the money spent for the war would be to create a new method of taxation, while at the same time lowering the level of discontent that was worming its way through the majority of the population.

This was why the council decided to pass a law in May 1427 for the land register system—a registry of properties belonging to all citizens that was based on the total wealth of each individual. A census of the wealth of the citizens was undertaken that excluded no one, by special council employees who wrote down every bit of information to formulate the total amount to be paid.

The less affluent segments of the population were immediately enthusiastic for the introduction of this new system, which they considered to be more equitable to their pockets.

Giovanni was remembered for this land register law. At the beginning he had been hesitant about the necessity to change the system in such a delicate moment for the council, but once he appreciated the hold that the register had on the people, he became a fervent supporter, so much so that he was willing to accept most of the praise for introducing it.

"It's a good law, Cosimo," Giovanni said to his son after the foundation of the land register.

"A great reform that is worthy of the financial novelties introduced by the past governments, Father," replied Cosimo, who still did not know well that change but trusted what his father was saying.

"Whoever lives within the territory of Florence and owns goods that make an income must pay taxes," explained Giovanni.

"All kinds of professional and business enterprises are considered goods," added Cosimo.

"Exactly," said Giovanni. "Only the income coming from manual labor won't be subjected to taxes—laborers will have to pay in a different way."

"What should be declared concerning incomes and possessions?" asked Cosimo.

"First of all, properties, lands, and buildings," continued Giovanni. "Then movable properties, animals, and finally any kind of money, even if invested."

"Is there anything else people will have to declare?" asked Cosimo.

"Of course," replied Giovanni. "All their debts and their other kinds of income. The tax inspectors will also have the power to request people to make an oath on the veridicity of their declarations." The law also had provisions for deductions for determinate entries, and the consultants used in each neighborhood of the city knew the state of the wealth of the inhabitants for that area.

There were special registers that dealt with particular categories, such as clerics or foreigners. But in all cases, the penalties for omissions or false declarations were severe.

In addition to penalties and prison, the right to vote was taken away from citizens who did not pay their taxes, and they could not appeal to any tribunal and were excluded from public office. This last point would play an important role in the future when Rinaldo would attempt to get rid of Cosimo.

In spite of the success of this new system, the situation was under the risk of degenerating between 1428 and 1430, when the Medici, and in particular Giovanni, were submitted to trials.

After years of tensions and tribulations, both Rinaldo and Niccolò were becoming increasingly aware of the concrete risk of the oligarchy losing power, and searched for solutions to at least relieve the situation. If Niccolò wanted to try to distract the citizens with some fiscal concession, Rinaldo had in mind provisions that were much more violent and drastic. He went so far as to consider revoking the constitution and have his city become his personal domain. Cosimo and Giovanni learned of Rinaldo's last decisions after a visit to Ilarione.

"I've spoken to a few of my messengers and what they told me isn't good," started Ilarione.

"Tell us everything. It's better to hear the news from you than to wait for the rumors to spread," replied Cosimo.

"Rinaldo called for a secret meeting in the church of Santo Stefano," replied Ilarione. "He wants to reinforce the more radical wing of his party with some new faithful allies, and he's also planning to halve the number of the Arti Minori in order to reduce the number of adversaries."

"He's surrounding himself with reinforcements to make sure the power stays in his hands," said Cosimo.

"Rinaldo would like to rule Florence with violence. What about Niccolò da Uzzano? Was he at the secret meeting or was he not told about it, just like me?" asked Giovanni.

"Niccolò wants to wait for your move," continued Ilarione. "He abhors every kind of violent action, but . . ."

". . . But he wants you to join them, Father, so that any possible rebellion will not have his most respected and sought-after leader—you," Cosimo anticipated him.

Even if Giovanni didn't participate himself to that secret meeting of the oligarchs, a few days later he received a visit from Rinaldo, who came to meet Giovanni and Cosimo at the bank's office.

"I know that your informers have already told you everything about the meeting, Giovanni," he began. After years of trying to get rid of the Medici, Rinaldo was making an unexpected attempt to attract them to his side. In doing so, he hoped to dissolve the danger that they represented by absorbing part of their prestige.

"Rinaldo degli Albizzi," said Cosimo. "Have you come here to tell us something new or just what we already know?"

"I want you to accept the conditions of my plan to reinforce my position of power. Right now, it's the only thing that would be good for Florence," said Rinaldo coldly.

"Is that what you are asking us? To go against the people?" replied a dumbfounded Cosimo.

"Your personal prestige will grow even more if you join my faction," replied Rinaldo. While his son spoke with Rinaldo, Giovanni remained silent, listening with folded arms; an expression of anger wrinkled his face, but not a single word crossed his lips.

"Fantasies! If anything, we would lose the prestige gained in many years of fair behavior!" exclaimed Cosimo, whose habitual calm was overtaken with irritation.

"You are less cautious than usual, Cosimo. However, you're not going against any law, and I can only advise you to lower your voice," replied Rinaldo in a threatening tone.

"We have had enough of this," Giovanni suddenly spoke, in a stern and martial voice. "Our answer is no. And now, Your Excellency, if you would excuse us, we have plenty of work to do here at the bank."

"It is either with me or against me," answered Rinaldo. "And I can see you've made your choice."

Rinaldo went toward the door, turning around one last time

to face father and son. "There will be new laws and decrees in the city, but I hope that this crisis will be over before anything can happen to you or your family," he said as he opened the door to the office. "I really hope so."

Rinaldo was not bluffing. He soon established a decree that forced all citizens to collectively swear twice on the Gospel that they would forget the tax issue and never undertake actions against the Signoria. Rinaldo even reached the point of commissioning a department to be in charge of verifying that each citizen had observed the new decree.

These were difficult times for Florence, but the situation calmed down especially when the land register was introduced, which, in spite of the praise given to Giovanni, ended up revealing itself as a great victory for Rinaldo, whose goal was to appease the spirits and strengthen the power of the oligarchy.

Although Rinaldo postponed once more his decision to hit the Medici, shortly after the family was upset by a tragic occurrence.

Chapter Six

A DEATH IN THE FAMILY

"*Miserere mei, Deus, secundum magnam misericordiam tuam.*"

"Pity for myself, O Lord, according to your mercy."

The Latin of the *Miserere* was marking the time of the funeral wake held in memory of Giovanni di Bicci, to whom Florence was bestowing the last possible honors before his burial at San Lorenzo, a church that Giovanni himself had contributed to with enormous financial aid.

It was the month of February in 1429, and Cosimo was at this point a middle-aged man, happy with his own family and secure in his career at the bank.

No tears rolled down his face, which was sad but inscrutable, while his family and closest collaborators came together in mourning before his father's dead body.

A desperate Piccarda was holding on to her sons while quietly crying and murmuring her own desire to die to reach in heaven the husband with whom she had spent her whole life.

Having aged to the point of being incapacitated by illness, Giovanni had prepared himself for death during the previous months, accomplishing his last good deeds and leaving farewell messages to all those who had been close to him during his life.

Cosimo was reflecting on the last moments that he and Lorenzo had spent with their father, and about his last words on his deathbed: "I have lived my life without offending anyone, but rather, trying whenever I could to help others," murmured Giovanni. "I leave you the riches that the Lord allowed me to gain and that I maintained also thanks to the help of your mother. Please, take good care of my Nannina and do not let my departure deprive her of the honors she deserves."

To pay homage to Giovanni, in addition to common citizens, representatives and prominent members of the major families in the city came to the service, names who inspired fear—the Rucellai, the Cavalcanti, and even the Albizzi themselves.

It had been a while since the latter were no longer guided by Maso, who died during the plague wave a few years before, but by his son Rinaldo, more impulsive than his father and always restrained by the old Niccolò da Uzzano in his hate against the Medici and especially toward Cosimo, his ancient childhood rival.

Some were kneeling on the praying benches, and others were standing in the shade far away from the center of the commemoration. Amongst many of these powerful people, hearsay and rumors were being whispered about the deceased and his family.

"Have you heard? They say that the funeral cost three thousand florins," said the young descendant of one prominent family.

"*At least* three thousand florins—a funeral worthy of a

prince. Cosimo spared no expense. Giovanni, however, managed to save enormous riches both through his business and his personal properties," replied the equally young manager of a rival bank with a hint of cynicism. "I'm sure he had already set aside the money for his funeral—even for ten thousand florins."

"Well, we should not forget that the funeral was worthy of a man who lived a just life and had the privilege to die in his own bed," proclaimed an old adviser, who could understand and appreciate better than those youngsters what kind of man Giovanni had been.

"I am sure that a man who dealt with so much money in his life could not be an entirely good soul. When someone dies, people only remember the best of them, but Giovanni was ruthless in pursuing the maximum possible gain from his enterprises," pressed on the manager.

"That is a quality that all good businessmen should have," reiterated the old adviser. "And Giovanni never charged high interest or practiced usury to become rich by gaining from other people's miseries. You seem to forget that Giovanni always tried to help people, both when he was asked to and out of the goodness of his own heart."

The young man nodded in agreement, causing the manager's irritation.

"But I say that . . ." the youngster tried to continue.

". . . That perhaps your venomous words against Giovanni might be dictated by the fact that, following the law, he requested that your business repay the debts contracted with his bank? Or am I mistaken?" concluded the old man. The arrival of Rinaldo degli Albizzi silenced the chattering, and a different kind of commentary started doing the rounds.

"Even Giovanni's enemies are paying homage to him, and this demonstrates that there can be greatness even in rivalry," observed the young man.

"Or perhaps Rinaldo is only here to make absolutely sure that Giovanni is really dead," replied the manager.

"Remember where we are and be respectful of this place," the old adviser admonished them again, then added bitterly, "Maybe Rinaldo is here to take stock of his new enemies. He's never liked Cosimo and now that also Niccolò da Uzzano is not far from departing his mortal coil, a clash between them is inevitable."

"What do you think Rinaldo will do?" asked the manager.

"He will get someone to advise them to focus exclusively on their bank, without trying to get in his way—or perhaps, he will tell them himself," replied the old adviser. "Even a powerful man such as Rinaldo must be aware that Cosimo and Lorenzo, with their wealth and intelligence, could easily extend their control on the whole of Florence."

The two young men nodded.

"Cosimo and Lorenzo, yes . . . or perhaps just one of the two," concluded the old man.

Leaning over his father's body for one last goodbye, Cosimo glanced at the three men. His expression changed, as if he had heard those conversations and already planned his personal future, his business's future, and that of Florence. As his mother and Lorenzo still knelt in front of Giovanni's body, Cosimo rose and turned as he heard a voice behind him.

"Your father was such a rare man. I remember that when the plague struck Florence again in 1417, the city would have mourned many more victims without his financial help and Christian charity."

Cosimo found himself face to face with Niccolò da Uzzano.

"And I know he'd have done the same even if he'd been the poorest of men," added Niccolò.

Niccolò was more cautious and wiser than Rinaldo. In spite of never having trusted the Medici's aspirations, he was a man who wanted stability in both business and life, and who now was asking himself if Giovanni's death would cause a shift in the Florentine political balance.

But most of all, Niccolò was wondering if Cosimo would continue in his father's footsteps or if he would look for a clash with Rinaldo. His ancient fears that despotism could take hold of Rinaldo and Cosimo had been stirred again.

"I am so happy and proud to hear such respectful words from you, such a respected man," replied Cosimo.

"Children often are an extension of their father's soul. I know this is true of you and your brother, Cosimo. And it is especially true when it comes to you," added Niccolò.

"I am afraid my mind could be dumbfounded on such a sad day. Allow me, then, to ask whether there's any hidden meaning behind your words," replied Cosimo.

"No hidden meaning," replied Niccolò. "I only know that after your father's funeral I shall retire to my study room to rest and ponder what the ascension to heaven of such a man will mean for us on earth."

"Whatever happens, it will always be in the best interests of Florence," concluded Cosimo, taking his leave from Niccolò with a slight bow of his head.

The funeral continued in the church of San Lorenzo, where Giovanni was to be buried inside a casket sculpted by Donatello in the center of the Sagrestia Vecchia which had been designed by Filippo Brunelleschi.

"Cry now, Florence. Cry, for this is the time to cover

thyself in sadness and pain." The funeral prayer that Niccolò pronounced moved everyone—family members, ambassadors, powerful and simple citizens.

Shortly after, Cosimo went into his father's office at the bank in order to immediately plan the next steps; with him were Lorenzo and Ilarione de' Bardi.

"Are you sure that to call to Florence all the administrators of our Italian and European branches won't be a waste of time, now that we must get reorganized?" asked Ilarione, whose usual sense of security seemed momentarily undermined by the mourning.

"It may seem a risky move, but that's what we need to save time while we reorganize the company and update all employees and administrators on the changes," replied Cosimo.

"It is because we trust you fully, Ilarione, that we're asking you to be directly in charge of this," remarked Lorenzo.

"Very well, then. I shall start taking care of it immediately," replied Ilarione as he exited the room.

Once Ilarione had departed, Lorenzo and Cosimo found themselves facing their cousins Averardo and Alemanno, who had arrived in town for the funeral and who were determined to push Cosimo to act against Rinaldo and take hold of Florence's reins.

"You and your father always had similar personalities, Cosimo," began Averardo.

Alemanno agreed: "He educated you and protected you by keeping you away from the political clashes of the last few years. But now, Cosimo, the time to act has come."

Lorenzo, who had been ignored by his cousins up until that moment, interrupted them: "You shouldn't consider only Cosimo. I, too, am similar to my father. If we have kept away from the recent clashes it's because he, although never remaining entirely neutral, never openly threw himself into the struggle for power."

Averardo tried to be more convincing. "With your riches and your influence, you could . . ."

Lorenzo laughed mockingly. "Are you talking to both of us now? Tell me, cousin, do you want us to change our entire attitude and modify the behavior we followed for years? And perhaps we should also risk our lives by becoming enemies of the most powerful men in Florence? I think this is . . ."

Cosimo stopped his brother with a gesture of the hand, then addressed his cousins with an almost servile tone. "Thank you for your suggestions. This is a day of mourning and we cannot focus on these matters with the necessary attention now. We will let you know our decision in due course," said Cosimo as he politely accompanied them out of Giovanni's office.

Once alone back in the room, Lorenzo addressed Cosimo with a scornful tone. "Are you seriously thinking to follow their advice and join the political fight just like that? What would our father say in seeing you act so recklessly?"

Cosimo took a deep breath before answering. "I trust them, and I know you feel the same way. That's why I think there's some truth in their words. We should think about becoming less unmovable, but . . ."

"But what?" asked Lorenzo.

"But, like our father would have done, we must be cautious, very cautious," replied Cosimo.

The situation inside the city seemed unchanged, but just as Niccolò sensed, the population and the highest representatives of society were consumed by doubt as they waited to see what would happen.

Cosimo chose not to show his face too much in public, and retired for a few days in the Careggi's villa, where he considered his strategy, and at the same time relaxed a bit with Contessina, Piero, and Giovanni. To expose himself excessively could put him and his loved ones at risk of assassination or attack by the most aggressive supporters of Rinaldo.

In the villa's courtyard, Cosimo and Contessina were throwing a small cloth ball back and forth, having Giovanni play by running after it.

"I'm glad you're spending some time with us, my beloved husband," said Contessina.

"You know how busy I am, especially now," replied Cosimo.

"I know. You do not have to apologize. We will not be the only ones to miss Giovanni; the entire city will too," replied Contessina. Then she added, "And I am aware of how much safer it will be for me and our children to spend these first days in Careggi, away from the city."

"You are a wise woman, my love. Meeting you has been one of the greatest blessings of my life," said Cosimo.

"Ah, you just see me like one of your bills of exchange, then!" replied Contessina with a piqued tone. Cosimo held her in his arms, caressing her face.

"You know I am not too versed in that kind of speech. However, it will be wise for me to stay here until I am absolutely sure that Rinaldo and his allies won't attempt something against me," replied Cosimo.

"Why would someone want to hurt you, Papa?" said little Giovanni, who stopped in front of his parents without them noticing.

Cosimo took his son on his shoulders, making him spin while kindly reprimanding him. "This little boy is always listening to what the grown-ups say—it is a sign he will become very intelligent." Becoming more serious, he added, "No one will ever lay a finger on me or any one of you. This I promise."

The next day, Ilarione arrived by horse to visit Cosimo and update him on what was happening in the city. From afar, Contessina noticed the dust cloud lifted by the man's horse. "It's Ilarione," she announced, unable to hide her concern.

"Don't worry," replied Cosimo. "He just wants to update me on the latest news. He wouldn't have come on his own in case of troubles. Keep on playing with our little one. I'll come back to you two as soon as I've finished with him."

Contessina nodded while Cosimo headed to the studio in the villa to prepare for the meeting. After welcoming Ilarione, Cosimo checked that no servants or laborers were eavesdropping, then closed the studio door and invited the man to sit.

"Where is Lorenzo?" asked Ilarione.

"In one of the other rooms, finishing a game of chess against Piero," replied Cosimo. "Don't worry, he will join us soon."

"Good. For my part, I took the liberty to instruct a messenger to come and tell us if there is any further news. You don't mind that, do you?" asked Ilarione.

"Of course not. And I believe I know what you're going to talk about. The new war against Lucca," replied Cosimo.

"Yes, you guessed right. A waste of money and resources, especially after all these years backing the war against Milan," said Ilarione, nodding.

"You're right. The Florentines backed this war because they thought it would have brought them easy glory, but now they complain they have to pay taxes to sustain the soldiers," said Cosimo.

"Easy glory and in exchange for what?" exploded Ilarione. "Nothing! Many were dragged into thinking that way after the quick conquest of a couple of castles in Lucca's territory by Niccolò Fortebraccio." Cosimo and Ilarione talked about the useless war that the heads of the city, who desired to increase their prestige, had initiated against the city of Lucca.

The motivations were not only inspired by a quest for prestige on Rinaldo's side, but were also tied to the backstage of another war, the one that had happened a few years before, in 1425—and the cause for much discontent. Florence had allied itself with Venice against Filippo Maria Visconti, Duke of Milan. Angered by the alliance between the city of Lucca's signore Paolo Guinigi and the Milanese ruler, once the war against Visconti had finished, the Florentine oligarchs hurried to get revenge by putting Lucca under siege.

"It's the presumption of being a great people that often pushes our fellow citizens, great and small alike, to think that way," continued Ilarione.

The war against Lucca would give rise to one of the most humiliating episodes in the long and glorious history of Florence, when Filippo Brunelleschi proposed a plan to expand the city by diverting the course of the river Serchio through a complex system of sluices and embankments. With a sudden strike, the people of Lucca broke the embankments, which made the water overflow into the fields of Florence, causing severe damage and taking numerous victims.

"We may be a great people but it's sheer stupidity to think of going to war without fighting or without paying a single florin," said Cosimo. "Believe me, I know only too well the sentiments people feel during a war, because I've had the misfortune of living through many of them, and I was even used as a hostage during a conflict with Pisa."

"I've been enough years on this land to intimately understand what you're talking about," agreed Ilarione. "Besides . . ."

". . . Besides, all these matters aren't healthy for business, especially concerning foreign merchants, who are more and more confused by this situation," anticipated Cosimo.

"Master Cosimo! Master Cosimo!" one of the servants shouted from the courtyard. "There's a messenger who needs to see you!"

"Send him up and allow no one to disturb me and my guest," replied Cosimo as he leaned out of the window.

The messenger ran into the studio, murmured something into Ilarione's ear, then handed him the handwritten note. Ilarione read it and addressed Cosimo.

"There's something else, I'm afraid. Fresh news."

"You look worried—what has happened? Quick, tell me!" asked Cosimo.

"You already know that Rinaldo degli Albizzi and Astorre Gianni are dealing with the war against Lucca as commissars," began Ilarione. Cosimo nodded in silence while Ilarione continued with his tale: "It seems that our soldiers, under Astorre's command, arrived in the village of Seravezza. The local people approached them, declaring themselves to be loyal servants of Florence, but . . ."

Ilarione wasn't able to finish—Cosimo interrupted, already guessing what the man was about to tell him: "They wouldn't have . . ."

"Yes," said Ilarione with a broken voice. "It's just what you're thinking. After feigning to accept their surrender, they closed all the inhabitants in the church and then destroyed and ransacked the village. Some survivors managed to arrive here and told us about the tortures and violence equally endured by both men and women."

No mercy for the defeated, thought Cosimo bitterly.

"For them and for nothing else, not even sacred places or virgin maidens," declared Ilarione.

"May those who committed such crimes be cursed in eternity. What do our citizens know about this, and how did they react?" asked Cosimo.

"Most of them heard the news and, thankfully, the majority are horrified and outraged," replied Ilarione.

"They may be horrified and outraged, but many wanted this war. This episode will forever taint and damage our city's name," replied Cosimo. "How could we blame Niccolò da Uzzano when he said that there could not be an endeavor more pointless, damaging, and expensive than this war against Lucca?"

"And even worse than that, we damaged a Guelph city that many times, regardless of dangers, welcomed Florentine Guelph who were forced to run away from the city," added Lorenzo, who had just entered the studio.

"Lorenzo, it's always good to see you," greeted Ilarione.

"Let us do away with the greetings, old friend," said Lorenzo. "I came upon your messenger—he told me everything. It appears times are even worse than we thought."

"We shouldn't forget that the soldiers paid by the Signoria lately are nothing but rural workers who don't want to fight but are only interested in pillaging and getting their salaries," said Ilarione.

"And without the help of mercenaries or foreign soldiers, the army we have now is mostly made of brutal cowards," reiterated Cosimo.

"You both are quite clear about the weaknesses, but we should have predicted how this would evolve a long time ago. It's too late now," replied Lorenzo.

"It's not too late to arrest and condemn Astorre Gianni and give back to the survivors what he and his men looted," said Ilarione.

"We shall start working to get some new war commissars elected," added Cosimo. "But we have to make sure that no candidate is related to the Albizzi family or their interests."

Cosimo was hoping to spread even further the feeling of indignation with regard to the events of Seravezza, with the help of the numerous messengers and *mestatori*, or mischief-makers, in his service. The latter were men charged to instigate the population and increase the discontent. The aim was to render the oligarchs' situation even more fragile. In spite of providing successes and economical prosperity, the oligarchs were witnessing the seething discontent from the inferior classes and from those citizens who, having had family members or friends who were exiled or cast into poverty during the decades of the oligarch's dominion, awaited a leader to help them rebel and seek revenge.

Cosimo sat at his desk and brought the palms of his hands to his eyes and reflected for a few brief, but intense, moments. "Tell me, Ilarione," he said. "What do the people of Florence think about my position on this war?"

"They are not inclined to forgive those who have caused this stain on Florence's reputation in the name of a war with no victory and no gain. And they're aware of your doubts on this conflict," replied Ilarione.

"But on the other hand," added Lorenzo, "Rinaldo says that most citizens are against this war just because you are inciting it. And there are people saying that . . ." Lorenzo hesitated while meeting Ilarione's gaze. They both knew what Cosimo's brother was about to say.

"Don't hide it from me, brother, because I don't want to fear anything from you, at least," Cosimo urged him.

"There are people saying you are the scourge of Florence, the cause of everything bad afflicting the city," replied Lorenzo.

"It's strange," replied Cosimo. "The first memory that comes now to my mind is a story my father told me when I was a young boy. It was the day they told me I was supposed to go to Pisa as a hostage."

"What tale?" asked Lorenzo.

"The one about our ancestor Giovanni de' Medici, who was decapitated under the regime of the Duke of Athens after being accused of not fighting properly in the war and of making a prisoner escape," replied Cosimo.

"What has it got to do with the current war on Rinaldo?" asked Lorenzo.

"It's quite simple. Even then, Florence lived under the control of a strong man who wanted to centralize all power in his hands. The war that finally caused the death of our ancestor was against the city of Lucca too. I wonder whether anything bad will befall our city again this time," replied Cosimo.

He took a deep breath, and after a few moments to collect his thoughts once more, he addressed Ilarione. "Make sure to meet all requests from whoever comes to the bank asking for a loan, or to ask for a favor, or to let us know that they cannot currently repay us. We must try to act in favor of our citizens, even more than we usually do."

"A wise decision, Cosimo," replied Ilarione.

"But how much will this 'tolerance' cost us, brother?" asked a worried Lorenzo.

"Certainly nothing more than what we spent on reorganizing our business after our father's death," replied Cosimo. "But above all, it will cost us less than what we would pay by turning Florentines into our enemies."

"I will record everything in the secret book, both expenses and losses," added Ilarione.

Within a few days, Cosimo received a new visit at the villa, a much more unexpected one than that of Ilarione. It was Luca degli Albizzi, brother of Rinaldo and an old acquaintance of Cosimo from the time of the hostage exchange during the war with Pisa.

The two toasted with a chalice of wine on one of the villa's balconies. It was the evening, and almost everyone at home was already in bed. The crickets of the countryside were the only company for the two old friends.

"Here's to you, my fellow hostage. If, indeed, those times will come back, let's hope it'll happen without too many unpleasant experiences," said Cosimo.

"To our health and to those who accompanied us during that adventure. May time give us the wisdom to remember with a smile even the most displeasing events," replied Luca, drinking his wine in one swallow. "It is excellent," he said, savoring the lingering taste. "Is this from your vineyards?"

"My father's," replied Cosimo. "It is the same wine we drank the day he decided to let Lorenzo and me run the bank. He was so proud of it that every year he sent a barrel of it to Niccolò da Uzzano. It became a long-standing tradition."

"I understand. And you? Are you keeping up with this

tradition?" asked Luca mischievously, knowing well the troubled relationship between Niccolò and the Medici.

"Niccolò might not have ever particularly liked my family, but he's a fair man. As opposed to . . ." Cosimo stopped speaking so as not to offend the guest.

". . . As opposed to my late father Maso or my brother Rinaldo?" asked Luca.

Cosimo sighed while putting an arm around Luca's shoulders. "My dear friend, our friendship was strengthened so many years ago and in such peculiar circumstances. I'd lie if I were to tell you that I am not worried about the situation with your brother and his allies. Furthermore, I respect your intelligence far too much to pretend that you know nothing of what is happening in our republic," said Cosimo.

"I thank you for your sincerity," replied Luca. "Likewise, I can only admit that I know what you're doing against the Albizzi and the other noble families. Even without exposing yourself too much and by simply declaring your enduring loyalty to the Republic and its government, you're ably stirring the people against Rinaldo and the aristocracy. This war against Lucca has served your purpose well and your bank will help you support and gain the loyalty of those who will go against the oligarchs."

"Luca . . ." Cosimo tried to interrupt.

"Wait, Cosimo, allow me to finish," Luca stopped him. "You will have a chance to speak. You're not just gaining people's sympathy through the clients of your *banco* but you're also helping private citizens, buying rare and expensive books for scholars and intellectuals . . . there are many other examples I could make. To put it simply, Cosimo, according to your friends, enemies, and the people in general, you come across as someone who would like to save Florence on his own."

"Why all these words, Luca? Are you accusing me of something? Have you visited me to betray our old friendship and the respect I thought you had toward me?" asked Cosimo.

"Quite the opposite," replied Luca. "Many citizens, through ignorance or greed, would be ready to betray and sell Florence out, but I would never put you amongst them. Besides, what have you done to stir my brother and his allies' suspicions?"

Luca took a book that was leaning on a chair.

"You use your money for things such as these, not just for your business. I wonder why the oligarchs complain about how you spend your riches. Is it perhaps forbidden by law to use them for either pious or magnificent reasons? Is it perhaps forbidden to use them to help people, to encourage scholars in their studies, to acquire ancient books, or even to lend money to common and powerful people alike?"

Luca gave the book to Cosimo, who started flipping through its pages, looking satisfied, before replying to his friend.

"And yet the oligarchs think of me as an enemy of freedom."

"They would know you don't possess the traits to be a tyrant, if they didn't fear the prospect of losing some of their power or even living a little more modestly," replied Luca. "And if some of them would look into the mirror, maybe they would understand what an enemy of freedom really looks like."

Those words confirmed to Cosimo that Luca had definitely shifted toward his side, as many other family members of representatives of the oligarchy had done during these last years. "Allow me to celebrate such beautiful words with another toast to the past," said Cosimo, raising his wine chalice.

"To the past and the future," replied Luca. The two friends raised a toast while the crickets around the villa chirped incessantly.

~

Time passed quickly, and a year flew by after Giovanni's death. Cosimo wanted his father to be publicly remembered with a sung mass and a solemn procession at each anniversary, in order to keep his memory alive among the people of Florence. During moments that they could spend together in the family home, Cosimo and Lorenzo tried to be close to Piccarda, who was growing increasingly inconsolable over her husband's death.

"Mother, please, you must remember how strong you've always been," Cosimo implored her, in vain. Piccarda spent her days in her husband's home studio, clutching to her breast Giovanni's most precious objects.

"I want to go to him. I want to be with him again. I pray to God every day that I will see him soon," she desperately repeated, almost as a lullaby. Cosimo lowered his head and, in the grip of intense discouragement, signaled Lorenzo to follow him outside the room.

"Do you think she'll ever get better?" asked Lorenzo.

"I would like to think so. I would like to have a grain of hope to allow me to lie to you and say that it will take a few months, and she'll get better. But if I were to do that, I would be disrespectful toward you both," replied a heartbroken Cosimo.

"So, what can we do now?" asked Lorenzo, glancing at his mother.

"Just try to make the time she has left as comfortable as possible. That is the only thing we can do and, believe me, it will be harder than seeing her die straightaway."

Piccarda died shortly after, in April 1433. Incapable of holding back the tears, her sons buried her together with Giovanni. They chose verses to be placed on the epigraph to commend the woman who had been so important to each of them and indeed to the whole family.

Chapter Seven

EXILED

The situation in Florence remained more or less stable for a few months, until in 1432 the bells of the city echoed again for the death of another illustrious citizen: Niccolò da Uzzano.

The moderate wing of the oligarchic party found itself without its leader, and his second most influential member, Palla Strozzi, had much less influence than Rinaldo, who in a short time managed to get back the reins of the whole party.

During the funeral mass, voices whispered gossip—intrigues and subterfuges spread while praying for the deceased.

"Poor Niccolò, he didn't deserve this insult before dying," declared Lorenzo to Cosimo—both were in attendance on the solemn day.

"Leaving almost everything he owned to improve the university, only to see his money used to finance wars or other useless endeavors," agreed Cosimo, shaking his head.

"A shame. What a shame," murmured Lorenzo.

"They say old Niccolò died of natural causes, but for a man

like him, I reckon that this last disappointment broke his heart in two," said Cosimo. He lifted his gaze and looked directly into the eyes of Rinaldo, who was watching him closely.

"Be careful, Cosimo. Your enemies' caution has died with Niccolò," Lorenzo admonished him.

The sentiment did not go away. Rinaldo and his oligarchs continued to plot and wait for the right moment to act against Cosimo, but they were forced to wait.

Rinaldo didn't seize the occasion even after the disappointment in April 1433, when peace negotiators gathered in Ferrara regarding the war against Lucca. It was April 21, and in Florence the citizens were still sad and discouraged because of that incapable leader and for that war that had only brought high costs and no results.

A few months earlier, Rinaldo had been nominated Roman senator by the new Pope Eugene IV, but that recognition just let him burn internally and consider himself a man only honored outside of his motherland. Yet, in spite of all of those letdowns, Rinaldo still waited for the propitious moment to act.

The war had continued with its opposing alliances. On one side, Florence and Venice were aligned, while on the other side stood Lucca, Genoa and Siena with the secret support of Milan. Interests were still high for every party involved but war during the Renaissance was a costly game, and now it was time to contain the damages or, most of all, the expenses, and put expansionist desires to rest. Presiding over the peace treaties was Cosimo, who had been invited along with Palla Strozzi.

"It's best the conditions for peace will not be too unfair for anyone," began Cosimo in front of the representatives of other cities. "And you must know that from this war, Florence has neither gained nor lost anything . . ."

The negotiations went on for several hours, but they found a resolution with excellent results, due to the oratorical and diplomatic ability of Cosimo. On the road back to Florence, Cosimo found himself talking with Ilarione, who had accompanied him for support.

"Rinaldo won't hold any public offices for a bit," said Ilarione. "My sources are certain of that."

"You always have your men ready to eavesdrop on any little secret in the *palazzo*, Ilarione. If I had a coin for every time you revealed something to me, I would be the richest man in Europe," said an amused Cosimo.

"I have never been so serious in my whole life, Cosimo. These past years' defeats have been too much for Rinaldo and I am certain that, after years of threats, this time he will really attempt trouble," replied Ilarione.

"Whatever he attempts will not catch me off guard—I have been ready all these years," said Cosimo.

Ilarione was right: Rinaldo continued to hesitate and continuously postpone the moment for revenge, but on top of the last disappointments, he felt also that a crisis in Florence was imminent, and had to find the favorable occasion to hit the Medici, once and for all.

After all, the conflict between the oligarchs and those who sided with Cosimo (these supporters were called *puccini*, because they were led by Puccio Pucci, a politician and old friend of the family) was affecting all aspects of life in Florence, including the cultural one.

An example of this had been the invitation to Florence sent to Francesco Filelfo, an important scientist and scholar of Greek and Latin, who had been called into the city from his native Marche to infuse further life into the local cultural scene.

145

Cosimo did a lot for Filelfo, both to make his stay in Florence a pleasant one, and to make him participate as much as possible in the city's cultural life. But shortly after, this man came into conflict with most of the other intellectuals, who accused him of being arrogant and envious as a consequence of feeling insufficiently promoted.

Being opposed by other intellectuals, among whom were several followers of Cosimo, Filelfo vented his anger with invectives and politically charged attacks, to the point of openly siding with Rinaldo and the other enemies of Cosimo. With the support of Filelfo, Rinaldo even started to think about transforming Florence's cultural scene, almost always devoid of political connotations of any kind, into a propaganda machine for his own image and for the oligarchic party.

In spite of the increasingly risky situation, Cosimo would not give up meeting with his intellectual friends, and often organized meetings in a cloister of Santa Maria degli Angeli. The participants of those meetings were the absolute best of Florentine culture, and when Poggio Bracciolini's duties in Rome allowed it (he had indeed been reintegrated into his old role of *secretarius domesticus* both by Pope Martin and his successor Eugene IV), he would also return to Florence to greet his old friend Cosimo.

While the other scholars spoke with each other, Cosimo took a few minutes to speak privately with Bracciolini himself. "How is your search between France and Germany going? Did you discover another monastery full of treasures?" asked Cosimo.

"I am searching across the whole of Europe!" exclaimed Bracciolini triumphantly. "And I am currently looking for something written by Archimedes."

"Archimedes? Original copies? I know this is something I

tell you every time we meet, but this might be your greatest challenge yet," said Cosimo, looking flabbergasted.

"Greek originals or medieval copies written in Latin. The ones translated by Guglielmo di Moerbeke are certainly easier to find. I hope," replied Bracciolini.

"As long as you will be in Florence for some time, don't forget you also have to read the newest additions to my personal library," added Cosimo.

"Oh, indeed, you did tell me about them in one of your letters, but I am not aware of most of your new additions. I know that you found something by Virgil and Livy, as well as inherited part of the fourteenth-century books owned by Roberto de' Rossi. There was also something by Petrarch and Boccaccio amongst those, correct?" continued Bracciolini.

Cosimo allowed himself to linger for a moment on his memories before replying, because certain books, like those that his ancient master had given him, reminded him of the happy years of his childhood.

"There is a book by Dante as well. But I want to ask you something else—how is Bruni? I have been told that you went to greet him as soon as you arrived in Florence. Did he tell you why he could not be here today?" asked Cosimo.

"He is working on his new oration, *De laudibus exercitii armorum*, and he does not want to leave his house until he's finished writing it. You know how Bruni is," replied Bracciolini.

"I know him and his character, but I have never heard about this new project. Did he tell you what it is about?" asked Cosimo.

"It is an oration he wants to recite in front of the Signoria and the citizens," replied Bracciolini. "A piece that will cover the past and present glory of Florence and illustrate how Bruni's humanism is also connected to the importance of politics."

Cosimo shrugged his shoulders while smiling. "The importance of politics, yes. Maybe even too much importance."

"Something troubling you, my friend?" asked Bracciolini, who still was not aware of all of the latest news.

"It is a long story," replied Cosimo. "You may not have heard of how things are evolving here in Florence. Rinaldo is always plotting something, and I have started to constantly watch behind my back. I guess you are not even aware of what happened with Filelfo . . ."

Before Cosimo could finish, a scream from one of the scholars broke the cloister's atmosphere of peace: "We want Filelfo to be officially denounced and be kicked out of Florence once and for all!"

"Well, I guess now you will know," Cosimo said to Bracciolini. All of the guests present at the meeting gathered around the scholar who had just shouted; the murmuring quickly transformed into exhortations to act against Filelfo.

"They even gave him a teaching position in rhetoric and poetry with a salary of two hundred and fifty florins per year!" shouted another scholar.

"Let us formally denounce him to show Rinaldo we are serious!" urged another.

Cosimo positioned himself at the center of the group, trying to appease the crowd. "I beg you, my friends, please calm down," he pleaded.

"You, Cosimo, of all people, are asking us to calm down?" retorted one of the scholars. "You, who has been the object of so many attacks and slander for so many years only on account of what you are."

Cosimo continued to try to calm the group. "If you know so many things about Filelfo, then you also know that Rinaldo and his allies have obtained for him a letter of immunity and citizenship rights."

"He is a scoundrel. I hear he even supports the Duke of Milan!" shouted the first scholar.

"Tempers are flaring, old friend," Bracciolini whispered to Cosimo. Cosimo did not want his intellectual friends to insist with this matter of pressing charges. Filelfo had become a symbol of the struggle between oligarchs and sympathizers of Cosimo, and pressing charges against him could cause serious political repercussions for Cosimo.

The situation did not resolve, and during the following two years, Filelfo became for all intents and purposes a spokesperson for the oligarchic party, publicly declaiming orations about Dante in which praise for the poet would be flanked with praise toward Rinaldo and attacks against Cosimo.

The moment for Rinaldo to act had definitely arrived, and in 1433 he managed to make his move, putting one of his own allies in the position of Gonfaloniere di Giustizia. The man chosen by Rinaldo was Bernardo Guadagni, who according to the normative of the law on the land register would not have been able to be elected because of his many fiscal debts. Rinaldo took care of "wiping his mirror clean," the expression used to mean erasing debt, bringing him on his side and maneuvering him to his liking.

In order to suppress possible uprisings in response to what he was about to do, Rinaldo also procured for himself the services of new armed men, who had come from outside and were not known to the citizens.

It was already summer, and Cosimo had decided to spend those hot months in his countryside estates. During the first days he found himself in his villa of Trebbio, in the Mugello, where news of Rinaldo's scheming had already reached him. A few weeks after, as if to follow Cosimo's relocation to another estate, those rumors would be definitively confirmed.

Cosimo, Lorenzo, Ilarione, and other members of the family found themselves together in the Mugello, in the Cafaggiolo villa, one of the most ancient properties of the Medici, dating back to the fourteenth century. At the beginning of the fifteenth, according to the land register, it proved to be a fortress belonging to Averardo de' Medici.

With the transfer of ownership to Cosimo and the intervention of the great architect and sculptor Michelozzo, the villa underwent further improvements. It was also loved by Lorenzo the Magnificent, who spent part of his adolescence there, and used it both as a gathering place for his circle of intellectuals and a retreat where he could write his works in peace.

When the convocation arrived at the villa through a horse-riding messenger, neither Cosimo nor his loved ones had doubts about the real motives behind it. "You must take the Passo del Giogo and flee to Bologna. You must save yourself," Lorenzo begged him.

"Lorenzo is right, Cosimo. Their intentions are clear enough. I hear rumors from my sources in the *palazzo*, and I can assure you that if you go there it might be the end of you," added Ilarione.

"No. It is not something I can escape from. My name is at stake, as is the name of the Medici," Cosimo replied, vehemently shaking his head.

"My love, please," Contessina begged him. "If you do not want to listen to what Ilarione and Lorenzo suggest, at least listen to me. Do not allow them to take you, for me and your children."

"I am a citizen and it is my duty to accept this call. They cannot accuse me of anything," continued Cosimo.

"You know how many enemies you've got in Florence, brother. Don't be naive. No one would respect or love you any less if you decide to do the only logical thing—avoid going and flee to a friendly city for a while," said Lorenzo.

"I do not fear my enemies, Lorenzo. Remember what our father used to say? To help everyone, not to hurt anyone," replied Cosimo.

"I just do not understand how a man of your intelligence and cunning," said an animated Ilarione, "both virtues you showed us plentifully during these years, could do something so crazy."

"What are you thinking?" added Lorenzo. "Are you relying on the Signoria to have sympathy for you?"

"I am relying on my innocence," replied Cosimo with an absolute calm. "I have not become stupid, blind, or deaf all of a sudden." Then, pointing at a chessboard made of fine inlaid wood, he added, "As a chess lover, you should understand my point, Lorenzo. I am like a chess player—I allow my enemy to move his pieces before moving mine. At the right moment, clearly."

"Then we will go with you. At least allow us to share with you what your fate could become," intervened Piccarda.

"I cannot allow this," replied Cosimo. "I told you, I will go to the Signoria on my own. You will stay here in Cafaggiolo, or feel free to go to one of our other houses. I just want you to be safe."

Cosimo also suspected what was about to happen to him, but probably did not realize the extent that Rinaldo had reached in order to put together his plan, nor the level of exasperation that had matured toward him over the years.

It was September 1433. Cosimo reached the *palazzo* the next day, a few hours after the pleas of the people closest to him. He arrived with his head held high, like a man who had committed no fault and was certain of his position and innocence.

Rinaldo, along with other members of the Signoria, sat and stared at Cosimo. A bundle with the list of accusations against him was promptly opened and read before Cosimo, who stood upright and attentive, after bowing in deference toward the men in front of him.

The bow was almost a mocking gesture, more a bow toward the grandeur of his city than toward the oligarchs who had finally made a move to ruin him, and who now were there, in total stillness, to enjoy what could have been the end of the Medici in Florence.

"Cosimo de' Medici, son of the late Giovanni di Bicci, are you ready to listen to the accusations the Signoria of Florence is presenting against you?" started the Gonfaloniere di Giustizia, Bernardo Guadagni.

Cosimo nodded silently.

"If you will be judged guilty, then justice will be done, and the bad seed born from your actions and riches will be eradicated from Florence," continued Guadagni. "The first accusation concerns the use of your money to pay your friends' debts in order to make them join your cause and turn them into enemies of the Republic."

Cosimo remained still, unmoved by that first statement.

The *gonfaloniere* continued with the list of accusations. "You've also lent money to other cities, princes, kings, or nobles who were not from Florence. And you have done all of this without any regard for the alliances and interests of our republic, or for the risks your actions could have caused."

Cosimo met Rinaldo's gaze, satisfied and full of hate: the two of them stared at each other for several seconds to prove that they were not afraid of one another. The *gonfaloniere* now named the final accusation: incontrovertible proof of Cosimo's tyrannical aspirations.

"Cosimo de' Medici, you are also accused of suggesting the war against Lucca so that you could take advantage of the consequences and subvert the Florentine state from within and put it under your control."

After this last accusation, a buzzing of satisfaction arose in the room.

"What have you got to say for yourself?" asked the *gonfaloniere*.

"I do not have anything to say," replied Cosimo. "I can only listen to your accusations and defer myself to the judgment of the Republic."

"Our state will judge you in fairness," concluded the *gonfaloniere*. "But in order to do this without risking your escape or you bribing false witnesses in your favor, you will await your sentence as a prisoner in a place you cannot leave."

"Let the *Capitano del Popolo*, the Captain of the People, enter," exclaimed Rinaldo while jumping on his feet. Accompanied by a group of soldiers, the captain entered the room, and without saying a word walked with Cosimo outside. From the corner of his eye, Cosimo noticed how Rinaldo and the others delighted in this scene.

"Take your time, signor Medici. Nothing to be afraid of," murmured the captain when Cosimo, still recovering from a bad episode of gout, was not able to keep up the pace.

But in spite of that kindness, Cosimo was trying to be even more cautious than usual. Not that he was afraid, but given the determination with which Rinaldo had managed to have him accused, not measuring his words or his actions in that moment could put his life in danger, and this was exactly what Rinaldo was hoping for.

Cosimo was imprisoned for twenty-seven days in the tower of the Signoria. That place had been euphemistically named *alberghetto* (small hotel) because of the not-too-delicate manners that were used with the prisoners, or *barberia* (barbershop) because it was once the place of work for the gentlemen's barber.

While Lorenzo, who was still in Mugello, considered if and how to gather the troops to travel to free Cosimo, the prisoner tried to spend his first days of detention in a peaceful manner.

The first part of the stay went by without any particular fear, but Cosimo started to seriously dread for his life whenever he heard the noise of armed men gathering on the square or, above all, the bell toll to call the population to parliament.

Even though he had made his move against Cosimo, Rinaldo found himself at an impasse. There were those who wanted Cosimo dead, those who wanted him to be exiled, and those who remained silent on the question. But because of the upright conduct Cosimo had always displayed, no one could condemn him for more than a few years of exile.

The Council of the Signoria met several times in order to decide what to do with Cosimo, but during the first deliberations they could only manage to establish that Lorenzo and their cousin Averardo should be exiled with Cosimo, as "disturbers of the homeland and very cruel enemies of the Florentine state." On top of this, a prohibition was declared against meeting or talking to Cosimo unless one had a written authorization from the Signoria.

Meanwhile, Cosimo began to be consumed by the fear of

being poisoned, and eventually he refused to eat. In spite of the dire situation, he established a friendly relationship of trust with his jailer, Federico Malavolti, a tall man with honest features, who was younger than Cosimo.

"Three days without food, Cosimo. I cannot force you to eat, you know that. But you cannot let yourself go like this," said Malavolti, seeing the bowl full of food that Cosimo had left once more.

"Thank you for worrying, Malavolti," Cosimo said with a feeble voice. "You are a fair man."

"I think the same of yourself and I know what you and your family have done for Florence. I am here only to do my duty. I have nothing against you," replied Malavolti.

Cosimo thought again about all the discourses on duty he had heard since he was a child: to do one's own duty at the bank, in his studies, and as a prestige hostage during a war between cities.

"I know what you are talking about. The man ready to do what his city orders him is often a fair man, unless he is blinded by hatred or desire for personal vengeance," replied Cosimo.

"Then why don't you make me a happy man and eat something?" the jailer said.

Cosimo looked at the food in the dish with an air of suspicion and disgust. "I cannot, unfortunately, and you know the reason. I have only got to wait. I will soon be a free man again."

Cosimo, weakened from tiredness and hunger, faltered for a moment; Malavolti helped him to sit on a heavy wooden chair that the jailer had allowed him in order to be more comfortable.

"You will not be able to wait much longer like this. Don't you understand there is nothing to fear from me?" asked Malavolti. "I am a less suitable man to poison you, and Rinaldo knows that.

I am just working for the Republic as a jailer. I do not double as a murderer." He then added jokingly: "Especially not your murderer, because you have not done anything against me."

"Thank you again, but I would rather be the one to decide not to fear for my life, and I am currently judging my chances of dying or living through this," replied Cosimo.

"Come on, Cosimo. You cannot really be afraid of dying with all the friends you have inside and outside the Signoria?"

"Friends *and* enemies. And as I like to say, life is full of surprises. Didn't you know that, Malavolti?" Cosimo replied with bitter sarcasm.

Days passed, and the indecision of the Signoria with regard to Cosimo's destiny was not only caused by the precautions of internal politics, necessary to avoid a revolt by those who were on the prisoner's side, but also by external interference of powerful Italians and Europeans who were asking in large number for Cosimo to be judged fairly.

The loudest of these voices were those from cities and powerful people with whom Cosimo had a privileged relationship of friendship or work. Support for Cosimo came from the Duke of Ferrara, as well as the majority of the powerful people of the Republic of Venice, where the Medici branch had a great importance for years.

In the *alberghetto*, Cosimo continued his strange friendship with Malavolti, who opened up more and more and by now considered the prisoner as a friend.

"Filelfo spoke against me during one of his public orations?" asked Cosimo.

"Yes. But things are getting better as well. Palla Strozzi managed to gather around him the few moderate oligarchs left, and they've all left Rinaldo's side," replied Malavolti.

"And the *gonfaloniere?*" asked Cosimo.

"He too seems less motivated than he initially was. I guess his gratitude wasn't eternal."

Only three friends received permission to visit Cosimo briefly, but the prisoner obtained at least the right of having food brought to him from home so he no longer had to fear being poisoned. In spite of this concession, a special functionary of the Signoria had the task of monitoring the preparation of the food in order to prevent anyone sending secret messages to Cosimo.

Cosimo and Malavolti got into the habit of eating together. "Your messenger told me he just got married to your cook, and added that if he doesn't fear being poisoned, you shouldn't be either," said the jailer jokingly, while carrying inside the cell a basket of freshly prepared warm food.

Cosimo was feeling more and more at ease with Malavolti, allowing him to bring one of his friends who wanted to meet Cosimo. The friend was named Fargagnaccio, and he was always ready to have fun and make jokes, just what Cosimo needed during those days of anguish.

One day at lunchtime, Cosimo addressed the two men to make them a particular offer. It was essential for him to speak with the *gonfaloniere*, and the only way to reach him was through Fargagnaccio and Malavolti.

"No, I can't accept any money, Cosimo. It would be a bribe, and I guess you understood the kind of man I am," said an indignant Malavolti.

"I understand and apologize, Malavolti," replied Cosimo. "It was not my intention to bribe you, it was just my only hope to . . ."

Malavolti suddenly stood up, interrupting Cosimo. "Enough, Cosimo. My duty is to serve the Republic, and there are things you cannot ask me to do." Then, without betraying any emotion, the jailer made a sign of assent to Fargagnaccio and went to the door of the cell.

"I have to be on sentry duty. I leave you with Fargagnaccio—I reckon you two could go back to that matter we were discussing," said Malavolti. The jailer could not have done more to help Cosimo without creating problems directly for himself.

"I . . . thank you, Malavolti. I told you already you are a fair man, but I can also assure you I will never forget what you've just done," said Cosimo with tears in his eyes.

"I am sure you won't forget. But you should also not forget that I will be back in a few minutes, so you better start talking as soon as I get out of this door. Did I make myself clear?" replied Malavolti.

Fargagnaccio willingly accepted the task that had been assigned to him by Cosimo, and with a good payment: leave the jail, withdraw some money on behalf of the prisoner, and deliver it to the Gonfaloniere Guadagni.

The *gonfaloniere* accepted with pleasure that "financial offer" (to which Cosimo added another big sum destined for a prior), and allowed Cosimo to have dinner to talk about his destiny.

"I can avoid your execution, but not your exile," said the *gonfaloniere* in front of a set table while handing some freshly baked bread to Cosimo.

"Would it be inevitable?" asked Cosimo.

"Inevitable," stated the *gonfaloniere*. "And I am afraid to tell you that it would have to last ten years. All to be spent in Padua."

"I hoped it would last less than that," replied Cosimo calmly. After risking death and seeing all of the family assets confiscated and redistributed, the news of the exile almost brought him relief.

"That is the most I could obtain from the Signoria. Or the least, I'd better say," replied the *gonfaloniere*.

"How will I get out of Florence? Who will come with me?" asked Cosimo.

"You will go with a company of soldiers. Incorruptible men, of course," said the *gonfaloniere* with a hint of cynicism. "So don't be afraid that they might have been bribed by one of your enemies. They will escort you out of Florence. Your children, your brother, and your cousin Averardo will follow you."

"I see. Thank you for sparing my wife the burden of leaving Florence. I wonder if you did that out of human compassion or to allow her to look after my business during my exile."

"Neither one nor the other," replied the *gonfaloniere*. "I just applied the law. I would have done the same thing for any other person with your same accusations."

The *gonfaloniere* opened the bag of coins that Cosimo had had delivered to him, and put his hand inside to feel the cold sensation of wealth.

"But, of course, perhaps not many other citizens would have had your same riches. Tell me, Cosimo, would you have guessed the material value of your life?" added the *gonfaloniere*.

"I guess I've pictured it to be costlier," said Cosimo while sipping from a cup of wine. "But I can assure you that I'd have given everything I own to get out of this."

"All your riches? That's because you know you would have earned everything back without batting an eye. Padua is in Venice's territory, and I am sure you won't miss this occasion to carry on with your business from there," replied the *gonfaloniere*.

"Maybe that is the truth, Gonfaloniere, but I will still be an exile sent away from his own city," concluded Cosimo bitterly.

Cosimo left with the other exiled on the night of October 3,

1433; he was joined by the architect Michelozzo, in one of the many demonstrations of loyalty that he gave Cosimo during his life.

While Cosimo was traveling further and further from the city, Rinaldo was reflecting on what he had just done. His was only an apparent victory, because he hadn't managed to have Cosimo sentenced to death, nor caused him a financial breakdown big enough to get rid of him forever. "If you must risk touching such a great man, you either change your mind or you make sure to annihilate him forever," Rinaldo said to his followers, who rejoiced for Cosimo's exile.

Moreover, Cosimo had been so prudent as to assure the most important part of his capitals by transferring them to branches of his bank or giving them to faithful friends.

Always escorted by the soldiers of the *gonfaloniere*, the exiled first stopped in Pistoia, where they were offered gifts, and then in Ferrara, where Cosimo and his comrades were joyfully welcomed by the citizens.

After reaching Padua, Cosimo received at the end of November permission from the Signoria to reside in Venice; Florence couldn't exempt itself from refusing the request of such a powerful allied city, while the *Serenissima*, or Republic of Venice, was hoping to obtain great commercial advantages through the presence of such a skilled businessman.

That was also the year Ilarione died. The death of a long-term skilled and faithful manager was another hard blow to bear, especially in such a complicated moment. The Medici Bank had lost another of its best managers, and it would take some time before they could find another one equal to the task.

Upon arriving in Venice, Cosimo met again with his brother,

who had preceded him during the final part of the journey by not stopping in Padua for as long as Cosimo. Lorenzo's exile in Venice was expected to last five years because of his attempt to trigger an armed revolt to free his brother.

"I know that Venice is safe from one Medici, but not from two!" exclaimed Lorenzo after embracing his brother again.

"Lorenzo! I knew you would arrive safely!" replied Cosimo.

"I've heard that every intellectual and man of letters in town is doing his best to render as pleasant as possible the exile of such a celebrated patron of the arts like you," said Lorenzo.

It was true. Since the first day he had set foot in Venice, Cosimo had received visits from many powerful friends, both old and new. "Don't kid yourself that they allowed us to be here together over Christian love, my brother. Even this reunion has been done in complacency to Venice's wishes. Even if it is certain that the most powerful men in this city hold us in higher regard of most of the ones in Florence," replied Cosimo, knowing that even their meeting again was the result of matters of foreign politics.

"Poor Ilarione. He would have really liked it here," Lorenzo said with extreme sadness.

"At least neither he nor our parents had to see how this story ended," bitterly replied Cosimo. "Just like they didn't have to see how Rinaldo tried to make our bank go bankrupt."

Indeed, during that first period of the exile, the Signoria tried to send into bankruptcy both the Florence and Roman branches by suggesting their clients withdraw their money. The plan failed miserably, given the financial solidity and guarantees that Cosimo was able to provide even in exile.

Cosimo also met with the doge of Venice, Francesco Foscari, who welcomed him like a prince.

"*Messer* Cosimo de' Medici," he said, having Cosimo rise from the bow he had taken to introduce himself. "Our Venetian Republic is honored to welcome you."

"Thank you, *eccellentissimo* doge," replied Cosimo. "Seeing that I had to be in Padua, it was my duty to come here to pay homage to your republic."

"And I hope that during your stay here we will be able to talk about the events taking place in Italy and Europe. I would very much like to hear your opinion on such matters, my dear Cosimo," said the doge.

"I wonder if I will be up to the task, doge," replied Cosimo.

"Oh, I am sure you will, believe me. We Venetians usually get along with Florentines. We are both merchants and business-men, knowing how important it is to understand what goes on in the world and to keep good relations with everybody," added the doge.

"But I feel the need to remind you that, at this time, I'm merely an exile," said Cosimo.

"Exile or not, I am sure you haven't lost your wisdom," answered the doge, "and being exiled didn't deprive you of the other branches of your bank in every city worth its salt."

Cosimo established himself in the Benedictine San Giorgio Monastery on the Island of San Giorgio Maggiore, a building with ancient origins where for centuries countless saints and powerful people had stopped.

"What are you bringing with you, excellent *signore fioren-tino*?" asked the abbot from the monastery, used to dealing with people of high rank without giving in to those who displayed arrogance.

"The gift of more knowledge," replied Cosimo. Based on a project by Michelozzo, Cosimo had a library built inside the old monastery (later destroyed by a fire in 1614) he had filled with a large number of ancient books, many also taken from his own private collection, which he had partially brought with him from Florence. Cosimo would have had part of the building structure restored, if they had not prevented him for doing so, out of humility.

When he wasn't working, Cosimo took walks around the city with his sons, who were now twelve and fifteen years old.

"As soon as we are allowed to leave Venice, the first thing you will do is return to your studies with your tutors," said Cosimo. "You boys just cannot seem to study properly here, and that is a shame."

"When it will happen, will you finally allow us to visit your workplace?" asked Piero, who was more curious to see how the bank actually looked inside and observe how it functioned, rather than begin his apprenticeship.

"Of course. But I have something in mind even better for you two," replied Cosimo.

"What, Father—what is it?" asked the livelier Giovanni, who by his nature reminded Cosimo of his brother when he was a child.

"You will work as apprentices in our branch in Ferrara. You will learn so much there, trust me," replied Cosimo.

"We will do as you say, Father, but when will we get back home?" asked Piero.

Cosimo put his hands on his son's shoulders. "I know, Piero. I too miss Florence, your mother, and our home. But you must understand that we have been beautifully received here, at a moment when our luck is at a minimum. And when a man's luck is down, most of his friends and allies often desert him."

"Giovanni and I understand what is happening, Father, but it is just . . . so hard," replied Piero.

"I understand that too, my son," said Cosimo, who then put his hand on Giovanni's head, caressing his long hair.

"What about you, *Giovannino*? How is life in Venice for you?"

"I am always bored, Father!" confessed the boy.

"But you are so lively, you would get bored on a battlefield!" exclaimed Cosimo. "Anyway, I want you to understand that even if we are living in troubled times, we have been allowed to live as we would at home."

Cosimo continued to show his magnanimity and influence by lending fifteen thousand ducats to the Venetian government for the resolution of some internal questions.

In the room where he spent part of his days studying and working, Cosimo was also busy sending and receiving letters to and from Florence, whose situation he was keeping tabs on with help from allies and friends who had remained in the city.

This way Cosimo also kept in touch with his wife, with whom he was communicating about their two sons' morale. And he learned that although Bernardo Guadagni and other allies of Rinaldo had obtained important positions for helping condemn Cosimo, Rinaldo was still criticized for banishing such a brilliant man, and not even a year after there was talk of allowing the exiled to return to Florence.

During that period, Florence hosted an illustrious character, Pope Eugene IV, successor of Martin, as well as a Venetian, who had been forced to flee from Rome dressed as a monk as a consequence of the pressure put on him by the Colonna family.

As these events were unfolding in Florence, Cosimo got

news of them in Venice, while he patiently waited for the moment of his return. During the first half of February, Lorenzo visited Cosimo, finding him more pensive than usual. "What is it, brother?" asked Lorenzo. Cosimo showed him a letter.

"Agnolo Acciaiuoli has been banished from Florence. He'll have to spend ten years in Cosenza," said Cosimo. In spite of being against the Medici initially, Acciaiuoli, a member of one of the most famous Florentine families and a man of some political weight, had approached Cosimo because he had no tolerance for the violent regime carried out by Rinaldo.

"What happened?" asked Lorenzo.

"They got their hands on a letter he wrote me."

"What was in it?"

"There is turmoil in Florence. People hoping for my return and . . ." Cosimo hesitated.

". . . And?" pressed Lorenzo.

"A suggestion to seek alliance with certain men of war, in order to have them by my side and use them to take Florence from Rinaldo."

"What do you make of it?"

"It won't be the right move to make. Violence always calls for more violence. We are playing a game of patience, Lorenzo. I will return. We will return."

During those same days, given Rinaldo's attempts to form an alliance with Milan, Cosimo is said to have attempted to buy the services of a Milanese *condottiero*, a mercenary captain, to attack Florence and cast doubts over the alliance that Rinaldo was looking for.

There is no concrete confirmation that this plot was hatched by Cosimo, who wanted to find the moment to return that would not risk compromising himself in any way; moreover, from letters sent to Venice by Agnolo and other allies of the Medici, Cosimo was well aware of the extent of the discontent in Florence toward Rinaldo.

The discontent was also growing among Rinaldo's very own political allies, as one after another were increasing the ranks of the Medici's supporters and trying to overturn Rinaldo before the situation could deteriorate into serious disorder or civil war. Among them was Neri Capponi, the son of Gino, who together with Luca degli Albizzi had shared the experience of being held hostage with Cosimo.

Months passed by, and while Rinaldo kept looking for external allies, and was seeing his own political weight growing lighter from the arrival of several allies of Cosimo in the new elections of the Signoria, a group of citizens sent a messenger to Venice to advocate for the exiled to come back into town.

The messenger and Cosimo were facing each other in the latter's room—a room worthy of a prince or ambassador, where Cosimo studied, worked, and received friends or dignitaries in peace. "No, I can't accept this," said Cosimo with his incontrovertible determination.

"It is a request made by a number of the most excellent citizens. Florence needs you, and they beg you to return as soon as possible," replied the messenger imploringly. "They say they will mount a revolt against Rinaldo and . . ."

"My answer is still no. I won't do anything without the explicit permission of the Signoria, therefore it is up to them to decide if I am allowed to return." In a certain way, Cosimo needed coaxing to accept a return to Florence. It wasn't a gesture dictated by arrogance, but more by being sure that all of those new allies wouldn't have betrayed or abandoned him at the mercy of Rinaldo's fury once he had finally taken a step back into Florence.

Shortly after, thanks to another ally's mediation, Cosimo got what he wanted when he received a letter with a favorable reply from the new Signoria.

Meanwhile, Rinaldo tried to ward off the situation with a plan to seize the Signoria by force, but on September 26, 1434, the day right after the fulfillment of the plan, the Signoria reinforced the guard garrison and had supplies brought to the palace in case of a siege. The Medici supporters had been warned in advance about Rinaldo's plan. He was now increasingly cornered, in spite of the repeated attempts to carry out a sudden attack with his most faithful men in arms.

As a result of his business and his privileged connections, Cosimo foresaw that he could count on the protection of Pope Eugene IV, who continued to live in Florence while waiting for the political conflict that had sent him into exile from Rome to find a resolution. Cosimo's intuition had been, once more, right. Aside from financial interests and his relationship with Cosimo, the pope had a political interest for Florence to be a stable government that could help him regain his place in Rome, thanks to an alliance against Milan between Venice and Florence.

During Rinaldo's last attempt to maintain control over Florence, the pope had summoned him for a meeting that lasted hours. Using his Christian faith as leverage, or maybe promising him that his attempts to maintain power would not result in extreme consequences, the pope was able to convince Rinaldo to desist from taking action with his soldiers.

On September 29, in Piazza della Signoria and in front of

a big crowd, a new *Balìa*, or ruling committee, formed by 350 citizens, was elected. The edict against the Medici was officially canceled after having been issued without a reason, praising the rectitude and behavior that Cosimo had maintained during his exile. On that same day, the Signoria decided to officially recall the Medici from exile, determining at the same time the deportation of Rinaldo, of most of his family, and of practically all of his allies.

Cosimo, Lorenzo, and almost all of the other exiled left Venice accompanied by numerous Venetian soldiers. It was September 30, 1434.

The group traveled through Ferrara, where it was welcomed with great honors by the citizens during the outward journey. The same thing happened with the city of Modena, which offered to Cosimo the protection of two hundred knights, whom he refused, possibly because he did not want to offend the Venetian escort.

Sitting on a cart during the lengthy horse ride and attempting to study some business documents, Lorenzo was shaking from impatience for the return, while Cosimo appeared absorbed in his thoughts and work.

"Happy about returning, my brother?" asked Lorenzo.

"We are still playing a game of patience, Lorenzo. Do not forget it until we sit in our own house in Florence," replied Cosimo.

"I know that, and I wish I could be as fearless as you are," added Lorenzo.

"Oh, it is not about being fearless at all," replied Cosimo, raising his head from the papers. "It is more like—how would our father say it? A combination of apparent modesty, lack of awareness, and . . ."

The cart jolted as it wheeled over a deep hole in the ground, making the two brothers jump up, interrupting Cosimo's talk. That moment brought back to his mind the many journeys made with Giovanni.

"Well, I guess our father would have said that there will never be enough holes for all the roads in Italy. And he would have added that the Romans could have built more of them!"

"More of what? Roads?" asked Lorenzo.

"Holes!" replied Cosimo with a laugh.

"What are you reading?" asked Lorenzo, trying to understand what was written in the letter that Cosimo held in his hand.

"One of the last letters I received from one of our friends and allies."

Lorenzo read it out loud. "Everything is crashing and burning. Poor Florence. God must help us."

Cosimo looked at Lorenzo. "You're wrong if you feel that I am not scared by what this return could become."

A military captain passed beside the cart in which the two brothers were traveling and leaned over to murmur something in Cosimo's ear. Cosimo nodded.

"What did he tell you?" asked Lorenzo.

"That several more soldiers are marching toward Florence right now," replied Cosimo. With the right amount of money, Cosimo had managed to secure extra protection for this return from exile. Now Lorenzo seemed more relaxed.

"We can feel a bit more fearless now, Lorenzo," said Cosimo.

Cosimo and Lorenzo did not return home immediately, but first stopped at the Careggi Villa, where Contessina and a few loyal friends were waiting for them.

"My love, let me hold you in my arms for an instant," said

Contessina while running toward him. Surrounded by friends and servants who rejoiced his return, Cosimo pulled Contessina toward him.

"Please, come inside. This house has been so empty without you, without all of you," added Contessina, prompting Lorenzo and her children to join Cosimo in the embrace.

"I cannot join you right now, my love," said Cosimo. "The boys can stay, but Lorenzo and I must go to the Signoria immediately. But I needed to see you and . . . change my cape."

"Change your cape, why?" asked Contessina.

"I will reach Florence after dusk, but I cannot risk anyone recognizing me—not yet, at least." It was October 5, 1434, when Cosimo finally reentered Florence. A year had gone by, but just as when he had left, it was at night when Cosimo came back. Just to be safe, in addition to wearing the cape and taking secondary roads, Cosimo's first night was spent in the Palazzo della Signoria, protected by numerous armed guards. There was still a lot of tension in the air, and even though the majority of citizens who heard of his return were jubilant, there was always the risk of an attack or that the last followers of Rinaldo who remained could attempt to incite a riot.

The day after, before retiring at last in his own home with his family and indulging in some rest, Cosimo visited the pope to thank him for the help he had given him with regard to Rinaldo. The two of them shared a mutual esteem, and Eugene did not care about the relationship that Cosimo had had with Pope Martin, a member of the Colonna family, who had chased Eugene from Rome.

Moreover, in order to make his stay in Florence even more pleasant, Cosimo offered to Eugene free use of all of his properties and any credit he wished at the bank.

"Raise your head, my son," said the pontiff when faced with Cosimo's respect.

"You did a great deed to me, Your Holiness," replied Cosimo, full of gratitude.

A big crowd, which had learned in one way or the other about Cosimo's return, began shouting and celebrating outside of the windows. "May God bless you always!" "Welcome back to Florence—don't ever leave again!"

"The only great deed I did is to Florence, Cosimo. And to the Florentines," said the pope.

In spite of being motivated by his own interests, those of the pope weren't only words suited for the occasion. Hearing the shouting and acclaims in his honor, Cosimo smiled.

"I will always do my best for this city and its citizens, Your Holiness."

"And they will always greet and honor Florence's favorite son, Cosimo."

When Cosimo took his leave from the meeting, he found Lorenzo waiting for him outside the door, joyful at hearing the people's acclaim.

"Do you hear them, Cosimo? Is it still a matter of patience? Oh, how I would like to see Rinaldo's ugly face now!"

"Now we go rest, Lorenzo," said Cosimo, patting his brother on the back. "I believe we earned the right to wait for tomorrow in our own home."

Cosimo had come back to Florence. The oligarchic dominion, which had lasted fifty years, was over. Rinaldo had been defeated.

Chapter Eight

ALLIANCES

The main members of the oligarchy who had not been exiled yet before Cosimo's return were either subjected to the same fate as their allies or were neutralized by sentences pronounced after various trials.

During those first days, Cosimo spent as much time as possible with Contessina, to whom he revealed his last decision.

"Moving to another house? But why?" she asked.

"You deserve a palace—you all do," answered Cosimo. "And I must confess that during the months I was forced to spend in Venice, I felt so conflicted between the desire of being in my home again and getting rid of a place with so many unpleasant memories."

"But we raised our two children in this house. This is where you let your beloved father stay so many times. This is . . ." Contessina tried to say.

"We will keep it for now, do not worry. It will take months

before Michelozzo will be able to finish the project, not even counting how long it will take to build it."

"Where will it be?" asked Contessina.

"I have bought a beautiful piece of land on the Via Larga. One of the last things I did before my exile. You are going to love it as much as I do, believe me."

After going back to work at the bank's headquarters, Cosimo received even more celebrations than he had already received upon meeting the pope.

As a first move, Cosimo paid out the debts of all of those who had remained loyal to him during the exile or lent them sums of money as a sign of gratitude. Then, together with Lorenzo, he started to think about changes to bring to the structure of the Medici Bank.

After Ilarione's death, and many years after the disappearance of Benedetto, the two brothers indeed decided that they wouldn't entrust the administration of the bank to members of the Bardi family any longer.

The decision was motivated by political games linked with the downfall of Rinaldo, or maybe to Ilarione's nephew, Lippaccio, whose talent was not equal to the task, and who had briefly worked at the bank after his uncle's demise. The new general managers were Giovanni Benci and Antonio Salutati, two experienced men with great abilities who had worked in the branches of Geneva, Basil, Venice, and Rome.

"You know you are taking after a great legacy," said Lorenzo, welcoming the two men who had arrived at the Florence branch.

"We know that very well," answered Salutati. "And will do our best to perform just as well as Benedetto, Ilarione, and Lippaccio," answered Salutati.

"Maybe not as well as Lippaccio," sarcastically added Benci.

Giovanni Benci was an unpredictable individual, an eccentric, aware of his own genius and capable of both a fervent faith and a vitality confirmed by his eight legitimate sons and an almost equal number of illegitimate ones.

Benci had been esteemed by Giovanni di Bicci, who had sent him to Geneva a few years before dying to oversee the creation of a branch of the Bank. "Easy, Giovanni," whispered Salutati, worried that Benci's joke could possibly anger Cosimo and compromise their promotion. "Remember your position and who you married."

Benci had married Ginevra de' Peruzzi, who was part of the historic family of Florentine bankers who had once been ruined by the English sovereign Edward III. The Medici had nothing against that union, but the Peruzzi had displayed hostile behavior toward Cosimo during the period of his exile, and the relationship between the two families was still in the process of healing.

"Don't worry, Benci. I have always appreciated sincerity. I would never reprimand a man for telling the truth . . . nor for the woman he married," said Cosimo, putting a hand on his shoulder.

The situation of the main branch and of the Roman one was good, but the same could not be said for the smaller branches, or for the merchants and producers who were working with the Medici. Now that his position on the social ladder was higher, Cosimo would do whatever was in his power to make the bank's businesses become even more prosperous.

"Shall we talk about the capital increase?" said Cosimo, changing the subject.

"From twenty-four to thirty-two thousand florins, just as you decided when we were still in Venice," replied Lorenzo.

It was the custom at the Medici Bank to encourage productivity and initiative among its most prominent members, so once they were promoted to general managers, Benci and Salutati also became associates of the whole company.

"Yes, thank you for reminding me," replied Cosimo. "Thirty-two thousand florins. Twenty-four provided by you and me as main partners and four thousand each from our new minority partners Benci and Salutati." The profits were divided in a different way; each one of the managers was given one sixth, as long as the share also included their salaries as manager.

"Cosimo and Lorenzo de' Medici and Partners," said Lorenzo solemnly, taking the contract to be signed by Benci and Salutati in his hands. "I will never get tired of reading that."

"Let us hope our two new general managers won't get tired of that either," added Cosimo, handing the inkwell to the two men.

Once the situation at the bank was solved, Cosimo found the time to meet again with his humanist friends, who welcomed him with great celebrations and laughter in the cloister of Santa Maria degli Angeli, where they often met.

"The prodigal son has returned from Venice! How many literary treasures have you brought with you this time?" asked one of the intellectuals.

"Plenty. And I will share them with all of you before the end of the day," replied Cosimo.

One man raised his empty glass to propose a mock toast. "Here's to Filelfo, an empty cup for a hollow man!"

Cosimo didn't push for Filelfo to be exiled, but the latter fled the city on his own once he heard that the exiled was on his way home. In spite of the hasty retreat, Filelfo once again tried to hinder Cosimo, writing a piece entitled *Discorsi contro Cosimo*, or discourses against Cosimo, so as to incite the last remaining oligarchs to revolt. Filelfo even threatened Cosimo with the publication of a book that attacked him further, asking him for big sums of money in exchange for it not to be published.

When he wasn't spending time with his wife, working at the bank, or discussing topics of interest with his humanist friends, Cosimo took time to sit in his studio to study documents and think in solitude.

And as it was a custom among the two brothers, Lorenzo could not help but ask what he was thinking about.

"Lost in your thoughts?" Lorenzo questioned. There was an air of disillusionment on Cosimo's face; the tasks and pressure of those first months after the exile had made him very tired.

"This is all a big riddle, my brother."

Cosimo had in front of him piles of documents in which the members of the Signoria were recommending or seeking advice about whom they should exile. Looking over all of those names, Cosimo was torn with doubts. How many had played their role against him? Who had done it because of being a true ally of Rinaldo and who did it only out of convenience? Who would have deserved a second chance and who deserved punishment?

Most of all, Cosimo wanted the true culprits to be dealt with just severity, but at the same time contain the spirit of the people and prevent mass violence or persecutions.

"Sometimes being too cautious will corrode you from within, Cosimo. Oligarchy is no more! The internal conflicts that plagued this city for the last two hundred years are gone!" said an excited Lorenzo.

"It can start all over again, and we might generate it ourselves," replied Cosimo.

"What are you talking about?" asked Lorenzo.

"I am talking about not letting the desire for revenge go over our heads."

"I see. You feel conflicted about sending Palla Strozzi into exile."

The leader of the moderate wing of the oligarchic party had just been sent into exile for five years in Padua. Palla Strozzi was already a seventy-year-old man, and that punishment would certainly mean dying outside of Florence. Cosimo's voice became colder.

"Palla Strozzi is a good man and a fair opponent. But this time he has been naive and misguided."

"But he finally left Rinaldo and his more fanatical allies for good," replied Lorenzo.

Cosimo knew that, in spite of belonging to the moderate wing of the oligarchy, Palla Strozzi was still powerful enough to undermine the basis of the new government in the hands of Cosimo.

"With the influence he still has, I would not want to risk his judgment slipping again. I am not the dreamer he is, nor a saint, but I know there could always be another Rinaldo," replied Cosimo.

"Why don't you suggest . . . more extreme solutions for him?" Lorenzo said with a provocative tone, knowing how averse his brother was to violence.

"Never," firmly replied Cosimo. "If I can help it, I will make sure no one will be condemned to death. It's true that a criminal wearing decent wool or silk can pass for an honest man, but it is also true that he who can judge men knows that violence is not the solution for everything."

Lorenzo thought for a minute about that reply, then came back on something that his brother had said shortly before.

"You just said you are not a dreamer nor a saint. What are you, then?"

"Right now, a man with many burdens."

"Cosimo . . ." Lorenzo tried to intervene.

"Listen, Lorenzo," Cosimo stopped him. "Our businesses, our banks, our name. We can use everything—and so can our allies—to seek revenge against our enemies. And yet we must avoid it. But in order to do so, we have to strengthen our power and that of those around us. This is the riddle. This is what we must do and also why we must be cautious."

"If this is all too much, you could retire quite comfortably, Cosimo."

"How? To live like I lived before being exiled? No, I cannot retire now. The town was on the verge of a civil war. We must keep on punishing the guilty, but most of all avoid having citizens going out in the street and start doing the punishing themselves. If we are forced to use violence against those who put Florence in trouble for their own interests, it will not be for personal revenge or hatred, but in order to have the city return to its former stability."

"If you want to watch over the city, then you could have the parliament give you a position of supreme authority. That could be a solution," said Lorenzo.

"I am not the Duke of Athens. Besides, I know our fellow citizens too well. Even if I kept being honest and incorruptible, the existence of a man holding all the power will quickly trigger discontent, conspiracies, and revolts. And that is the last thing I would ever want."

Lorenzo replied in a more mischievous way, making a joke that only a brother like him could indulge in. "And you would not have time for your businesses."

"I am a businessman, I am a banker, I am a man of letters, and I am a Florentine citizen who loves his city more than he loves his own life. I am so many things at once and I still must master how to make all of them live together inside my body and my mind."

Cosimo was considered the governor of the city, and it seemed that both the Signoria and the population really wanted to bestow upon him a title so that he would manage Florence like a supreme ruler.

"Remember what our father and mother taught us," reaffirmed Cosimo to Lorenzo. "Never attract too much attention, and never partake in the race for power." Following this advice, Cosimo refused to govern Florence openly, but from behind the scenes, counseling and making decisions through a few trusted men.

Walking on his own through the roads, a habit he hadn't lost even during his exile and which he had inherited from his father, Cosimo could understand more and more how Giovanni must have felt every time he strolled along the streets of Florence.

"When can I visit you? I have some urgent questions!" demanded an old merchant.

"Welcome back to Florence, dear Cosimo!" shouted a girl.

"Would you like to be the godfather of our first child?" asked a young couple.

Just as it had been for Giovanni, those displays of reverence and affection weren't only meant to demonstrate that Cosimo was a just man, but also how big his importance had become in Florence. In that way, Cosimo understood that in spite of not holding any of the highest offices in the government, the citizens offered him their eternal loyalty.

Cosimo thought that he could guarantee the stability and

security of the city by maintaining all of the constitutional institutions, and by continuing to act from behind the scenes. The Florentine political structure would undergo no substantial change, and to confirm this continuity and the sense of the state, Cosimo held the office of Gonfaloniere di Giustizia for two months in 1435.

But in spite of that concession to political life, Cosimo was concerned about behaving as much like a private citizen as possible, acting through his most trusted men to hide his important personal influence. At his side, in addition to his brother, there was the faithful Puccio Pucci, who together with Cosimo analyzed the political situation by studying strategies.

"You want to allow the aristocracy to have the right to vote?" Pucci asked Cosimo.

"Yes. It won't count as a great reform, but it is something that might pull some weight," replied Cosimo.

"I do not understand the reason, though. The nobles have not been complaining about this. I think you should let sleeping dogs lie."

"No, quite the opposite. This change will leave a good impression on the people and make everybody happy. The citizens will see that the great noble families have finally understood the need to embrace democracy, while the nobles will see it as a reward for not siding with Rinaldo and his oligarchs during my exile."

"Are you telling me you want to risk putting nobles up for important public offices?" Pucci asked hesitantly.

"No, not for the time being, at least. For the moment their eligibility will be purely theoretical, and their names will never actually be included in the ballot boxes," replied Cosimo, showing as usual his extreme realism.

It was due to these types of concessions and small changes that Cosimo consolidated his power in Florence. Still, in his meetings with Pucci, Cosimo also expressed the desire to create a new social class in Florence, a middle class (his detractors would rename it "mediocre"), made of the "low" members of the citizenry, so insignificant in the social ladder that they weren't even eligible to be members of the *arti minori*.

"And we would distribute some public offices to the most deserving of these so-called small men," said Cosimo.

"But never in the history of Florence have men of low social standing been allowed to occupy public offices," replied Pucci. "What can we hope to gain with this move?"

"First, it is necessary to redistribute power to the entire population," answered Cosimo. "Secondly, by doing that we will strip the few oligarchs who have not run away or have not been exiled of the little power they still have. Furthermore, that is how we will gain new allies, especially amongst the people, and avoid the risk of being overturned by the wealthiest, most power-hungry members of the arts."

Most of the families who had been exiled under the oligarchy were now back in the city, some having been away from Florence for decades. Cosimo was particularly satisfied about these returns. However, sometimes even he had to resort to violence. Coming back with Lorenzo from the funeral of their cousin Averardo, Cosimo and his brother found themselves discussing precisely this matter of extreme punishment.

"I shouldn't say this, but in a way I am glad Averardo is no longer with us. Caution left him during his final years," said Lorenzo. Cosimo didn't reply. He was thinking along the same lines as Lorenzo, but every death of a friend or family member upset him profoundly.

"Once he returned from the exile, he let his personal hatred go to his head."

"The main thing is to avoid falling into his same mistakes," added Cosimo. Lorenzo took out the envelope with the new arrangements from the Signoria; Cosimo was still in the dark about that matter and, for once, his brother had anticipated him.

"Have you heard that there will be two public executions soon?" said Lorenzo.

"What?" said Cosimo with alarm.

"It is all written here. Read it." Cosimo read it quickly, but in the note, there was only a mention about the crime committed by the two convicted.

"What are their names?" asked Cosimo.

"Bastiano and Riccio. We don't know much about the latter, but he seems to be a Spaniard," replied Lorenzo.

"And they tried to kidnap the pope from Florence to bring him to the Duke of Milan in order to use him against our city?"

"Yes. As you said, a bit of wool or silk can make a man mistake a villain for a good man."

"How will these two criminals be punished?"

"With what Florence has always given to men of their kind—public execution by decapitation."

Cosimo took in a long breath. In that case the death penalty was inevitable and, for the seriousness of the crime and the standards of that time, even justified.

"It is of capital importance to increase the power of the magistrates in order to make them more efficiently face Florence's internal enemies. Perhaps, if we manage to improve the situation in the city, we will have fewer of these external conspiracies and attacks," said Cosimo hopefully.

In addition to increasing the power of the magistracy, and

in spite of Cosimo being rightful and honest by nature, he made use of other means to get rid of dangerous opponents. He imposed particularly heavy taxes and controls of the land register for those who could obstruct him. Often in these cases, opponents ended up ruined and forced to leave Florence, or their possessions were confiscated by the government and divided among Cosimo's allies.

Cosimo also ensured that public offices would not be held by sympathizers of the remaining Albizzi, and in order to do so he made use of a technique also used by his enemy, which involved the maneuvering of the "matchmakers" who took care of the names to elect, leaving out disliked or dangerous names.

Cosimo considered all of these actions necessary for the well-being of the city. Florence may have needed a true and proper reform of its constitution, but that was not so simple. First to prevent this was the confidentiality with which Cosimo managed the situation of the Republic. Moreover, to the conservative and distrustful eyes of Florentine people, each reform of the state bodies would have been seen at that moment as an attempt to impose personal power.

It did not matter the extent to which almost all the people of Florence esteemed Cosimo. At the slightest suspicion, whether true or false, that Cosimo wanted to make a personal dominion of the city, the citizens would start a revolution.

Cosimo often talked about it with Piero, by now a young man who was increasingly involved with city matters. As promised by Cosimo during the exile, Piero and Giovanni spent most of their time in Ferrara learning their trade at the bank's branch there.

Piero was having lunch with his father and mother at home,

and was also taking a small rest because of the pains caused by the gout, which already ailed him.

"I am glad you're back for a few days. It will also be useful for Giovanni to be on his own for a little," said Cosimo. "How is it going in Ferrara? Are you and your brother learning?"

"We are, but our tutors and supervisors are relentless," answered Piero.

Cosimo was giving his sons the best possible education, in both studies and work, just as he and Lorenzo had received from their father.

"They better be—that is what I pay them for!" joked Cosimo, who suddenly became more serious. "But tell me, what do they say about Florence in Ferrara?"

"Oh, Cosimo, let him rest for a bit. His foot caused him great pain," Contessina intervened.

"I will, as soon as he tells me," Cosimo added jokingly.

"You know your father," said Contessina, caressing Piero on the head. "I suggest you answer him if you want to get him off your back for a few minutes!"

"People in Ferrara are . . ." Piero hesitated, still too immature to talk in depth about political matters.

"Well?" pressed Cosimo.

"Well, some people I have spoken to asked me about our taxes. They say it is unfair the way they're distributed," Piero finally replied.

"That's because they don't know they are equally distributed. More than that, actually. Everyone pays, but the rich pay more than the poor."

Cosimo was referring to the novelty of the progressive tax on ascertained income, an innovation that had been welcomed with great approval and that allowed a more equal distribution of tax among social classes.

"Will you explain to those people what I just told you?" added Cosimo while he ate a piece of bread.

"But what should I tell them if they ask how it is to live in Florence? Some of them are confused, and they don't know if people are free."

"Of course we are free, Piero. Florence is a democratic republic!" said Contessina.

"Your mother is right," said Cosimo while cutting more bread. "Florence is still a republic, but when the situation calls for it," he added, "we must use any means to create a functioning government that leaves behind useless political quarrels."

"What is the worst thing that could happen to a state, Father?" asked Piero.

"Incessant internal clashes make a state die slowly, and that is what we must avoid."

"So why don't you ask the Parliament to give you supreme authority like uncle Lorenzo said?"

"It is not my attitude and, above all, it is not necessary. I know very well how Florentines think and, like I told your uncle, my hypothetical rise to power would lead to discontent, lies, and conspiracies in a very short time."

"What is your objective, then?"

"The safety of Florence, the defense of our territories, not surrendering to any threats. And then, of course, the development of culture, architecture, and art."

"This is why we need to change our constitution."

"No, this is why we need to keep it as it is, at least for now, and also why I have become a *gonfaloniere* for two months. We must seek the support of the people, and we won't do so by changing everything, but by keeping it working as it is, as best as we can."

Cosimo tried to stay true to his words. During the course of the years he also sought to establish occasional decrees concerning the statute of citizens and the complex laws of corporations, but the legislative situation in Florence continued to remain complicated.

Those taxes came out of a conflict that had been taking place intermittently for more than ten years. In spite of the peace agreement in Ferrara a few years before, Florence had returned to dealing with the war against the Duke of Milan, Filippo Maria Visconti, who was trying to seize Tuscany at all costs with the aim of extending his dominion over the whole of Italy.

Cosimo found himself analyzing the events with Puccio Pucci and Neri Capponi.

"How do you see this situation, Neri?" began Cosimo.

"Potentially difficult. Our expenses have already been high enough, but we'll have to spend more to hire capable soldiers," replied Neri, whose competence in the art of war, which he had inherited from his father Gino, had become fundamental for Florence.

"But how will we get the money?" asked Pucci.

"If necessary, we will call for a special tax," said Cosimo.

"The citizens might start thinking that you are looking to drain their pockets dry to improve the city's finances," replied Pucci.

"I am aware of that," said Cosimo. "And perhaps somebody will think that this is just a subterfuge to impoverish the wealthiest families. But everybody will have to understand that with the current taxation system, the more you have, the more you pay—and my family is among the ones who pay the most."

"It won't be easy getting everyone to understand that. There's still a minority talking behind your back. Survivors of Rinaldo's old regime," replied Neri.

"Rinaldo, Rinaldo," mumbled Cosimo. "Despite all his flaws, he and his oligarchs always regarded defending the Republic against external enemies as a matter of life and death."

"Their loyalty toward Florence has always been unquestionable," added Pucci.

In reality, as it would become apparent later, the banishment of Rinaldo and his comrades had cooled their patriotic instincts, something neither Cosimo, nor Neri, nor Pucci could be aware of. The pressing matter of the moment was to find a *condottiero* capable of defending Florence, or at the very least one whose fame would be great enough to deter Visconti from attacking the city.

"I have an idea," exclaimed Cosimo.

"And a name in mind?" asked Pucci.

"Yes. There is a man who could help us save Florence, a miracle worker when it concerns the art of war. But we must bring him here first," replied Cosimo.

Neri, who knew the majority of the *condottieri* all around Italy, gave him a questioning look. "That can be done, but who is this miracle worker?"

"And what will happen then?" added Pucci.

"Allow me to see to it," replied Cosimo.

And so it happened that between 1435 and 1436, Cosimo cultivated a new friendship that changed the course of Florence's history.

The miracle worker was Francesco Sforza, son of a *condottiero* who had died by drowning a few years before and from whom his son had inherited both position and nickname, namely "Sforza" because of his physical prowess.

He wasn't sophisticated in the same way that Cosimo's men were, but he was equally astute and maybe more ambitious and unscrupulous. Sforza had already fought at the service of the Duke of Milan, who wanted to use the ability of the *condottiero* for his desires of conquest, promising him in exchange his daughter's hand, and in so doing making him the successor at the head of the duchy.

But in reality, Sforza was looking at his own interests and, because the relationship with the paranoid Visconti was increasingly complicated and the promise of marrying his daughter was postponed every year, Sforza sought out other alliances that could give him more guarantees and allow him to obtain an increased personal prestige.

Not everyone in Florence welcomed that piece of news. In Cosimo's office at the bank, Lorenzo threw a pile of documents on the floor out of frustration for his brother's decision.

That was perhaps the first time Lorenzo openly criticized one of Cosimo's decisions, possibly pushed by the bad mood caused by the worsening of the illnesses that afflicted him.

"Can you please calm down?" asked Cosimo as he bent to gather the papers on the floor.

"I am sorry," replied Lorenzo as he took in a big breath to try to find some calm again. "But I don't think you have made the right choice this time."

"How so?" asked Cosimo.

"You are not thinking about present and future alliances," replied Lorenzo. "If you bring Sforza on our side, you will make an even meaner enemy out of the Duke of Milan, who will assume you have plotted behind his back to rob him of his most valuable *condottiero*. And you will also make an enemy out of the pope, who has already had enough problems with Sforza when he tried to conquer some papal territories."

Lorenzo's hypothesis wasn't implausible, and most of all, antagonizing the pope could bring not only potential problems for the future alliances of Florence, but also to the Medici Bank in his role as main pontifical bank.

"Your points are valid," replied Cosimo. "But you are forgetting that, right now, Sforza himself has turned against the Duke of Milan. For what concerns the pope, I am sure he will turn a blind eye to Sforza's past if he will help him against Visconti and solve his problems in Rome."

"You are basing your conjectures on ifs and buts," answered Lorenzo.

"Then allow me to read you something." Cosimo took a dusty container full of old documents, extracted one, opened it, and started to read. "'My dearest friend, I am glad that our cooperation is growing more productive by the day. I will soon be in Bologna with my firstborn Cosimo . . .'"

"What is this?" asked Lorenzo.

"It is one of the many letters our father and Baldassarre Cossa exchanged. You remember what you thought of him, even when he became pope, don't you?"

"Of course, I do, and I also remember how you made me and our father stop arguing that day at the thermal baths. But I do not understand why you are mentioning Cossa. Are you trying to compare him to this pope and Sforza?"

"Not at all. I am simply pointing out another of our father's lessons that we should always keep in mind. When it might be worth it to run a risk, one must be ready to count on people we would not normally trust."

With the Signoria's approval, Cosimo invited Sforza to Florence, where he was welcomed in 1436 with honors and celebrations.

Sforza was a man of great physical prowess, dark curls, and facial features worn out by a difficult and dangerous life. In spite of everything, and even if he didn't have Cosimo's culture, Sforza was also a man of a sensitivity who was looking for support and friendships outside of his line of work as a *condottiero*.

Escorted by Neri Capponi and by Cosimo, the *condottiero* was moving with difficulty among the crowd of citizens. The Piazza Santa Croce was crowded with Florentines, who were going back and forth between that spot, which was the center of the knightly games, to Piazza della Signoria, with its performances of dancing women.

"A fantastic display of grace and power," said Sforza, who attended the knightly games organized in his honor by Cosimo.

"A small, necessary tribute. Florence knows how to celebrate its worthier guests," replied Cosimo.

"We hope you will join us in our alliance against Milan. We will also have the aid of Venice and . . ." Neri tried to explain before two jubilant children swooped down on him.

Sforza burst out into unrestrained laughter. "If even your young boys possess such ardor, then my choice of joining Florence has been wise! We shall win any war!"

Cosimo moved away with unsuspected agility in order to avoid being swept away by the children who were running along the square. Sforza looked at him, surprised by such a swift movement.

"That is something I never expected to see—a show of quickness by the esteemed Cosimo de' Medici, known to all for his intelligence, his business skills, but also for his rather frail health . . ."

"Life is always full of surprises, dear Francesco," replied Cosimo. "And most of the time, it is things we never expect."

Even someone as disenchanted as Sforza was flattered and honored by the almost paternal behavior that a man like Cosimo could show toward him. It was because of this special treatment that the *condottiero* was convinced to take advantage of all of his tactical flair for the cause of the league anti-Visconti, of which he had been named general captain.

In spite of that positive beginning, things with Sforza didn't exactly go as Cosimo had foreseen. Nevertheless, during those months Cosimo was busy with other matters, mostly related to his banking and to his relationship with Eugene IV.

On March 25, 1436, the day of the Annunziata celebration, Florence was the scene of a solemn celebration for the end of the refurbishment work of the Duomo, where the dome designed by Brunelleschi many years before was finally completed.

Pope Eugene, who was leading a solitary ascetic life inside the Florentine Laterano, decided to bless the building and the whole of Florence, offering as a gift to the new church a golden rose, the most important symbol of papal honor. For the ceremony, Brunelleschi himself had built a bridge that went from Santa Maria Novella up to the Duomo, covered with blue and white cloths upon which the pope and his cardinals could walk.

Once the celebration was over, Cosimo went to Santa Maria Novella to have a private meeting with the pope, though not in his official capacity but as a simple Christian penitent. Just as when he came back from exile, Cosimo wore a humble cape to meet the pope to keep from being recognized by anyone.

That precaution was so efficient that, once he arrived in Santa Maria Novella, the cardinals accompanying the pope hesitated to leave the pontiff alone with the mysterious visitor.

"I need some time alone with this man," the pope told his cardinals. "Leave us. I guarantee you he will not do me any harm." While murmuring about what the pope commanded, the cardinals readily left the room; Eugene signaled Cosimo to remove the cape.

"So, I was right," said the pope. "It is the same cape you wore when you returned from your exile."

"That is right, Your Holiness," answered Cosimo. "And I thank you for conceding me a few minutes of your time." In spite of having kept it secret from his loved ones, by now it had been some time that Cosimo's own conscience was eating him away inside.

"I have always tried to do my best for Florence," began Cosimo. "But like every other man who has to deal with politics, I feel I have tainted my conscience on more than one occasion."

"What is troubling you the most?" asked the pope.

"I feel that some of my riches have been earned in an unfair way, Your Holiness." More than Palla Strozzi's exile or the other expedients that Cosimo had used to safeguard his own position, he looked in anguish at the money he had earned through his bank, or that he had maybe taken away from more or less honest citizens through very high taxation.

"There is a thin line dividing what is wrong from what is right. Like you said, you've always aimed at the greater good for Florence, and very rarely at your personal advantages. But if you feel the need to shut down these thoughts you are having," replied the pope, "then I guess you will have to give back the money you feel you have earned unfairly."

However, if moral law was asking Cosimo to give back that money, how would he establish to whom it should be given? Should it be given to the exiled? Maybe to those amongst Cosimo's enemies who had left Florence after having been sent into bankruptcy by the land register? Or maybe to some merchants through whom Cosimo had earned more than he should have by taking advantage of the currency exchange or favorable markets?

"That's what we will do," established the pope. "Your penance will be to 'bury' ten thousand florins within the Dominican friary dedicated to Saint Mark."

With that periphrasis the pope offered Cosimo to employ that money to restore the ancient convent, which had been used in the past by Celestine monks as a form of penitence. The pope, who resided just outside of Florence along the Via di Fiesole in the convent of Saint Dominic, had recently assigned the convent to the Dominican Order.

"I shall accept the penance," replied Cosimo. "And I shall put Michelozzo in charge of the works."

"If it will be half as beautiful as the dome built by Brunelleschi, I will be incredibly pleased," replied the pope.

"In order for you to be, Your Holiness, I shall spare no expense," added Cosimo. "I will actually tell my administrators to sign all accounts and expenses needed without even showing them to me."

"I can already picture how it will look. It will be a splendid penance for a divine goal," concluded the pope.

In this way, Cosimo was able to hush his conscience, and in the end, he spent forty thousand florins for the restoration of the convent and the church, more than quadruple what the pope had asked of him. But in spite of solving his moral and spiritual doubts, another problem soon presented itself to Cosimo. Indeed, inside the Signoria's rooms, Cosimo, Neri, and Francesco Sforza discussed the next moves that the latter should undertake.

Sforza was conscious of his value as a *condottiero* and was increasingly annoyed by the uncertainty and disunity of the cities that were part of the anti-Visconti league, and not a day passed without him thinking about the benefits of that new alliance.

"Taking Lucca?" asked Sforza. "Ten years after I have defended it from your troops. You are right, Cosimo, life is full of unexpected surprises."

It was a paradoxical situation. A few years before, Sforza had truly fought for Lucca during the war, the cost of which had been used as an excuse to send Cosimo into exile. Moreover, this time Cosimo's feelings toward the conflict were very different. This time, in fact, Cosimo felt that with the current status of the war and the pace in which Visconti was fighting his enemies all over Italy, Lucca could have become one of Milan's more useful strongholds to conquer Tuscany piece by piece. And maybe, as opposed to violence as he was, Cosimo even considered this decision as a move to boost the citizens' morale with a military victory.

"It is imperative that we take the city," said Cosimo decidedly.

"If I remember correctly, you were against Rinaldo when he attempted to take it years ago," replied Neri.

"You are correct," replied Cosimo. "But back then it was a conflict aimed at finding easy glory, and quite unfair to the good deeds that many citizens of Lucca did for the Florentines. And I am also sure you remember the view of a wise and respected man like Niccolò da Uzzano expressed on that war,"

"Even at the time, Visconti was watching Lucca's back," said Neri while Sforza silently observed some military maps.

"Then let me say that, this time, the situation seems far more dangerous," answered Cosimo. "If Visconti manages to exploit Lucca for his plans, Florence will be in serious trouble."

"They might accuse you of wanting to take Lucca to increase your personal prestige, like your ancestors did with Pisa," said Sforza, who already understood the way in which political games worked in Florence.

"Or perhaps they might even accuse you, Cosimo, of wanting Lucca in order to put your friends and allies in positions of power there," added Neri.

"You are well aware, I hope, that both these accusations are not true," replied Cosimo. "But having said that, before we come to a conclusion we also have to hear what our other allies think."

"I planned this ahead of you," intervened Sforza. "And I know that Venice wants this bit of the war to be fought across the Po Valley. They've got plenty of cities there they wish for me to take."

"Everyone puts his own interests first," replied Cosimo. "And Venice wants the control of those areas to increase its commercial gains."

"What do you want me to do, then?" said Sforza, annoyed by those plannings and delays. "Whose orders should I follow? I could have already moved the troops, but you're all so uncertain!"

"Lay siege to Lucca. Sooner or later the city will fall. And let us pray that there will be very little blood shed on both parts," said Cosimo.

Lucca did not capitulate, in spite of the long siege waged by Sforza, who managed to conquer only minor territories of lesser importance around the city.

Sforza was increasingly disillusioned, and under Visconti's reiterated promise of letting him marry his daughter, he allied himself again with the Duke after a series of secret negotiations. This piece of news reached Cosimo in advance by means of one of the many messengers he had in his service, a habit he had inherited from Ilarione to anticipate both adversaries and allies.

"Cosimo! Cosimo! He betrayed us! Sforza betrayed us!" shouted Neri as he suddenly entered Cosimo's office at the bank.

"I know everything already," said Cosimo, inviting Neri to sit and calm down. "But perhaps you are the one who does not."

"He accepted a new alliance with Visconti in exchange for his daughter's hand, that traitor!" continued Neri.

"No, that is just a part of it. Sforza renewed his alliance with Visconti on the condition of marrying his daughter, but he also asked for a clause to allow him to keep fighting for us. By the same token, the Duke promised not to attack Florence."

Cosimo took from the drawer a pitcher of special wine that his father used to love and offered Neri a chalice. Having come out unscathed from his very first argument with Lorenzo, he would also come out unscathed from Neri's agitated reaction.

"Have you calmed down now?" asked Cosimo.

"Too many emotions in a single day. I'm afraid I am getting old," replied Neri.

"*We* are getting old," replied Cosimo shrewdly.

The matter involving Sforza hadn't yet found a definitive

resolution, and the *condottiero* would play an important part in the future of Florence. But in the meantime, Cosimo immediately fixed that small failure by bringing one of the biggest events of the century to Florence.

Indeed, a few years earlier, and more than ten years after the Council of Constance, Pope Martin V decided to open a second council in Basel, Switzerland, to continue the reform of the Church, solve the problem of the Hussite heresy, and most of all, attain the union of the Western Latin Church with the Oriental Greek one.

The desire to unite the two churches did not only come from western religious officials; the Byzantine throne was indeed threatened by the constant pressure of the Turks, and Emperor John VIII Palaiologos had been forced to ask powerful westerners for help, giving in exchange the ability to negotiate a reconciliation of the two churches.

Pope Eugene IV took the reins of the council in his hands once Pope Martin died, and Cosimo himself invited some employees to Basel to open a branch of the Medici Bank, just as had been done in Constance.

But a few years after the opening of the council, the continuous conflict between the conciliar movement and the pope had become intolerable, forcing the latter to move the event to Italy, resulting in the convergence of a great number of members of the Eastern Church to the peninsula.

Cosimo was in his villa of Careggi to help his servants plant new fruit trees. In spite of being weak and ill, working in the fields and doing humble work on his estates made him feel good.

Coming closer to a luxuriant fruit tree on the estate, Cosimo couldn't resist asking one of the youngest laborers the same question that Roberto de' Rossi had asked him when he was a child.

"Come here, young man," said Cosimo, signaling the boy, an adolescent with red hair and a curious face.

"Yes, signor Medici?" asked the young man, taking off the hat he used to protect himself from the sun as a sign of respect.

"How old do you think this tree is?" asked Cosimo. "Older or younger than Florence?"

The young man looked at the tree and tried to seriously reply to Cosimo while repressing his laughter for such a strange question: "Oh, but signor Medici, this tree is barely ten years old. You should know better than that!"

Amused by the pragmatism of the boy's reply, who was too involved with the difficult daily reality of manual labor to think in terms of conjectures and abstractions, Cosimo signaled him to rest and eat something from the big table full of food that had been set for the workers under the shade of one of the balconies.

Lorenzo arrived shortly after to announce the news about the new council to his brother. He was limping, and his face was pale and looked thinner.

"Did you hear, Cosimo?" asked Lorenzo. "The pope wants to move the new council to Ferrara. Do you remember when we went to Constance?"

"Ah, we were much younger back then. Bracciolini, Bruni, poor Ilarione. That was quite a journey," replied Cosimo with a nostalgic sparkle in his eyes.

"And getting married as soon as we returned," added Lorenzo.

"How are your sons doing, by the way?" asked Cosimo.

Lorenzo pretended not to hear that question. His sons were very different from the way he and Cosimo had been as young men. They were not very interested in studying and were more devoted to the worldly pleasures of life.

"I think the pope should have chosen Florence, though," said Lorenzo.

"I wonder if we can still do something about it," replied Cosimo, whose mind had already started working. Lorenzo's intuition had lit the latest spark of genius in his brain, namely to convince the pope to move the council from Ferrara to Florence.

It was an honor to host one of the biggest religious events in the world. Cosimo and the people of Florence wanted to bet on the potential of the new council and knew that they could exploit the union between the two churches—not only for spiritual exchanges, but also cultural, political, and commercial ones.

Cosimo asked for a meeting with the pope, who was getting ready to open the council in Ferrara. The year was 1438, and for a long time the pope had continued to reside mainly in Florence.

"Without your presence, the Lateran won't be the same," began Cosimo with his cultured and pleasant ways, which had fostered the friendship with Eugene.

"Oh, do not worry, my child, I will get back here every time I can. Ferrara isn't so far away, as you know," replied the pope.

"Not far at all. But if you want to know my opinion, I say Florence would be the most suitable city to host the council."

"You know how much I love Florence, but would you care to tell me why?" replied the pope.

"Fair enough. Its location, the comfort of its accommodations, the abundance of food, and, if I might say so, the generosity of its inhabitants and the peace the city has enjoyed lately."

"I know about all of that, and you are always convincing.

But I gave my word to Ferrara and I cannot take it back. Are your children still working at the bank there?"

"They are spending time in Florence. Their formation at the bank is not going as I hoped, and they shall be better tutored here," replied Cosimo, referring to the limited ability in preparing for business displayed by his sons. "But if you change your mind, Your Holiness, consider my proposal as a way to repay the deeds you did for me. I will also guarantee you a loan of seventy thousand florins and the ships to bring here the Greeks who have not yet arrived in Italy."

"I will remember your generous offer, Cosimo," concluded the pope. "I certainly will."

Florence continued not to resign itself to that refusal from the pope, not even when the council was officially opened in Ferrara. Again, fate smiled down to Cosimo and to his city. Because of a sudden wave of plague and of the continuous threat of one of Visconti's *condottieri*, Pope Eugenio decided after reflecting at length with his retinue to accept Cosimo's proposal and move the council a third time.

Back in the Careggi villa to celebrate the news with his family, Cosimo also met again with Lorenzo, whose appearance seemed to have even worsened since they spoke for the first time about the new council.

"You did it again, Cosimo. I thought you had softened a little after what happened with Sforza, but I was wrong," Lorenzo told him, giving him a hug.

"Thank you, my brother, but we have also been lucky once again," replied Cosimo, noticing how unwell his brother looked. "But now tell me about you—are your maladies still not giving you a single moment of peace?"

"That is how it is, I am afraid," replied Lorenzo while coughing. "This time I feel the pain in my bones. Even though I am still fairly young, I feel my body is that of an old man."

Cosimo was also ailed by arthritis and gout, but Lorenzo's sudden worsening was serious, and his cough seemed to foreshadow an ominous future.

"But you still possess the soul and the mind of a young boy," Cosimo said, trying to ease his worry. "You will soon get better. And don't forget, I need your support for the council to run smoothly. I know you will not disappoint me."

Lorenzo and Cosimo hugged again, both unaware that that would be one of their last conversations.

On January 27, 1439, the pope returned to Florence, an occasion celebrated by Cosimo, the Signoria, and the entire population.

"I told you I would return soon, my child," said the pope.

"The Lateran is waiting for you, Your Holiness," replied Cosimo.

"Yes, but do not forget your promises," reiterated the pontiff.

"I will not forget them. I never do. The expenses for your return have been paid by Florence, and we are already restoring and improving Santa Maria Novella."

"Excellent. I knew you would keep your word. And concerning our other matters . . ."

"Don't worry—I have been thinking about everything you asked for and even more. Florence will be glad to provide a home to our Greek guests without asking for money. And we're also ready to give them a monthly allowance for their petty expenses."

"Thank you, Cosimo. You are generous, but also aware of what you will gain from the money you're spending."

"You know me well, Your Holiness."

"And I remember equally well the day you came to confess. Do not worry, this is well-spent money, and it will give blessed fruits to the Medici, Florence, and the Church."

Constantinople's patriarch arrived in Florence on February 12, accompanied by a vast retinue of prelates and monks, all dressed in the fashion of their countries, a curious spectacle for the people of Florence, who rushed to witness the arrival of the foreigners.

"Father, Father, the Greeks have arrived in Florence!" shouted the young Giovanni running into Cosimo's office at the bank to inform him.

"They've arrived early—thank you for warning me. What do you think of them?"

"They are the strangest foreigners I have ever laid my eyes on, Father. Some of them have long beards and disheveled hair, others have short beards and shaved heads with painted eyebrows!"

"How did our fellow citizens react?"

"Some laughed at the sight of such strange people, Father."

"What about you, Giovanni? Did you laugh as well?" asked Cosimo with a serious tone.

"No, I did not."

"So, your teachings are bearing their fruits. One should never laugh at those who are different, especially if they come from a great civilization. Remember, Giovanni, that even if their appearance might seem strange, these Greeks are often more dignified than many of the priests we have here."

On February 16, the most important guest arrived, Emperor John VIII Palaiologos. He was hosted in the Palazzo Peruzzi, built on the perimeter of an ancient Roman amphitheater, and curiously close to one part of the city called Borgo dei Greci, named because of an Orientalizing colony that had arrived in the city in ancient times to sell ointments and perfumes.

The emperor was a man of great charm, tall, with a long neatly trimmed beard as was the Greek custom, and dressed in Damask brocade clothes, with a headgear from which protruded a precious jewel.

Dressed more modestly, as was his custom, Cosimo introduced himself to the emperor with all the affability he was capable of. "I have been told you are a man of utmost importance," said the emperor to Cosimo.

"People exaggerate, especially Florentines," replied Cosimo with his usual combination of modesty and caution. "I am just a businessman, and in my spare time I attempt to be a man of letters."

"Ah, that is even more interesting to hear," replied the emperor. "Then you will have much to discuss with the many scholars I have brought here to your country."

Remembering also the pomp seen during the Council of Constance, Cosimo spared no expense, welcoming the guests with a magnificent ceremony and providing them with the best possible stay during the months of duration of the council, hosting them in the most sumptuous palaces of the city and amusing them with parties, dance performances, and shows of all kinds.

The Greeks appreciated every bit of the Florentine hospitality, even when it was more of the humble variety, such as eating unfamiliar dishes like pork chops, which they savored in the inns of Florence, shouting *Arista*, meaning "such a good thing." *Arista* would remain the name in Florence, and the majority of Italy, for that kind of food.

"Try this wine," said Cosimo to Bessarione, the solemn head

of the Greek luminaries, at the end of a banquet. "We only make it here in Florence, using dried white grapes."

"It is just like the wine from Xantos!" exclaimed the luminary, referring to the similarities between the Florentine wine and the one made on the Greek island.

"Saint wine?" asked Cosimo, who in the noise of the banquet barely managed to hear his guest. Just like the *arista*, from that misunderstanding the people of Florence would continue to call that traditional wine *vin santo*, roughly translated as saint wine, a name that lasts to this day.

Months passed, and the sudden death of Joseph, the patriarch of Constantinople, risked slowing down the council. But thanks to the emperor's predisposition and to a new note found in the patriarch's room in which he had written that he recognized the supremacy of the Roman pontiff over the whole Church, the council ended earlier than expected.

"Heaven and earth should rejoice," declared the pope at the end of the last meeting. "For the wall dividing our two churches has finally fallen, and we will now have peace and harmony again!"

Cosimo stood up to applaud together with the religious authorities of both churches. "There is always light after darkness," he murmured to Lorenzo, who had managed to drag himself with great difficulty to that meeting. The union between the two churches was short lived, but it also meant another victory for Cosimo, because the council had not only promoted Florence's industry and commerce, but because of the meeting among scholars from all over the world, it also gave a new impetus to the humanist movement.

Indeed, that meeting between scholars and intellectuals of

the Greek and Latin schools generated a great fervor for Greek philosophy, especially the Platonic one, considered by the humanists as the origin of Latin knowledge, which they searched for up until that moment.

When they were not busy with religious arguments, Greek intellectuals were discussing with the Florentine humanists Homer and Virgil, Plato, and Aristotle. Although he was thrilled by all of those new cultural drives, Cosimo was fascinated especially by the figure of Giorgio Gemisto, named Pletone, an authority on Platonic philosophy. By listening to the speeches with which he entertained the Italian intellectuals, Cosimo rediscovered the passion for the great Greek philosopher.

Turning once again toward his brother, Cosimo murmured, "I want our city to become the new Athens," a promise he would have kept at any cost.

Chapter Nine

THE NEW ATHENS

After that event, Cosimo was once again forced to take care of the conflict with Visconti and of the question of alliances of Florence. In spite of the tension and very high taxes imposed on the citizens in order to sustain costs, Cosimo understood that the continuation of that war would paradoxically bring benefits to Florence.

The whole of Italy was shaken by conflict, and Cosimo wanted to take advantage of this to modify Florence's alliances. The city always had associations with Rome and Venice against Milan and Naples, but Cosimo felt that changing things could be very convenient—to both oppose Venetian competition in commerce on Eastern markets and to exploit the power of Milan and its very powerful lords.

However, to implement his politics in regard to Milan and Venice, Cosimo would have to wait for the death of Milan's lord, Filippo Maria Visconti, who, among several changes of mind with Sforza and the feeble attempts to install peace, kept trying to invade Tuscany and take possession of Florence.

In this case, someone stoked the fire and pushed toward a new invasion, a man Cosimo thought he had defeated for good.

"Visconti is being incited by one of your old enemies," Neri Capponi told Cosimo during an emergency meeting in the Palazzo della Signoria.

"Who is behind this?" asked Cosimo. "Maybe Filelfo? Or perhaps Palla Strozzi? That would make him a wolf in sheep's clothing."

"The answer is simpler. It is Rinaldo," replied Neri.

"The hen is laying his eggs!" murmured an adviser into Cosimo's ear.

"He won't manage to lay them if he pokes his nose out from where he's hiding," replied Cosimo with a joke.

It was 1440, and not even ten years after Cosimo's return from exile, Rinaldo and his exiled comrades were trying to encourage Milan to take back Florence by force and reorganize the oligarchic party. That action wasn't entirely unexpected. It was normal for the exiled sometimes to go against their home city, becoming in the process rebels who risked incurring severe consequences.

Indeed, by moving away from the place that had been designated for the exile without an official permission, such men were liable to incur the death penalty with the accusation of high treason.

"Exiles never sleep," said Neri.

"Of course they don't," replied Cosimo with another joke, "I've taken sleep from them myself."

"Rinaldo must be certain that if he manages to move

Visconti's troops toward Florence, our citizens will revolt against you and welcome him back," added Neri.

"We will see to his foolish dreams," replied Cosimo. "After all, we still have one special weapon."

Cosimo was referring to Francesco Sforza, who had once more come back in full service of the anti-Milanese league because of his grudges caused by the unfulfilled promise of Visconti to allow him to marry his daughter.

After a few battles with various results on both sides, Visconti's soldiers moved onto Florence, but once they arrived beyond the Mugello, they waited in vain for Rinaldo's prophecy to come true, and for the people of Florence to welcome them by chasing out Cosimo.

"We are already organizing the defenses," said Neri with determination.

"Are the citizens afraid?" asked Cosimo.

"Yes. Visconti's troops are among the finest in the world, and they know it. But we are much more resolute in fighting for our homes."

The descent of the Milanese troops found its final resolution in the battle of Anghiari, where Florentine militia chased away the soldiers led by Visconti, who, even before the battle, had already gotten on the road home to Lombardy.

The failure of Rinaldo's sudden attack was the last nail into his metaphorical coffin: a sentence of infamy.

Cosimo and Lorenzo witnessed this sentence by stopping outside of the *palazzo* for that ritual, which had been the same for centuries. Rinaldo and his comrades were given a judgment by default for the death sentence, for being outlaw rebels and enemies of Florence. Their portraits were put on display on the walls of the palace, along with their with names and faults written in block letters, so that all citizens knew that they had betrayed Florence.

That sentence was worse than the death penalty, because it was also followed by the confiscation of their possessions and the loss of all of their rights.

"We have had our victory," said Cosimo to Lorenzo.

"But you surely do not think that condemning Rinaldo once more is the solution to all our problems," replied Lorenzo.

"I was not talking about Rinaldo. Visconti will not try to attack us again. Now it is time for the peace treaties and to discuss the future."

The peace treaty between Visconti, Florence, and Venice was signed in 1441 in Cavriana. That same year, in Cremona, Sforza reentered into an alliance with the Duke by finally marrying his daughter.

Visconti wasn't dead yet, but with Sforza's wedding with the Duke's daughter, Cosimo could already start to spin his web to ally himself with Milan. Even the commercial nature of Florence was going through a transition. In the factories, more waves of foreign workers were arriving from countries such as Holland and Germany. In 1440, along the streets of Florence, fights between laborers of high and low Germany were recorded. One road where many German laborers lived was nicknamed *la via tedesca*, meaning "the German street."

Cosimo administered the city of Florence from behind the scenes, and as usual participated in some of the council deliberation, where he did not impose his decisions but acted like any other member. The banking activities were doing well in their commerce with the East, but the bank's dominant position with the English and French courts was by now a distant memory.

But one prominent member of the Medici would not have

time to witness the new changes in town nor the peace with Visconti.

In 1440, Cosimo was shaken by yet another terrible loss. His beloved brother Lorenzo died at only forty-five, plagued by the family illnesses that by then had made him feeble and aged. His death left inside Cosimo a new enormous and unbridgeable void.

"I would like to help you make the arrangements for the funeral, my love," said Contessina, seeing her husband more dejected than ever at home.

"I would not want any other person by my side, but this I must do alone," replied Cosimo sorrowfully.

"But perhaps having someone you love by your side would be the only thing helping you right now," Contessina tried to insist.

"No, not this time. When we go to spend a few days in the countryside, it takes us weeks to prepare for our stay. In this case, it is up to me to prepare Lorenzo's soul and body for a dark journey from whence he shall never come back." Several years later, Cosimo would pronounce those same words when he felt close to death himself.

During the organization of the funeral, Cosimo asked to meet Poggio Bracciolini, who, during that period of working with Pope Eugene, was often in Florence.

"You do not realize how saddened I am," said the man while coming toward Cosimo to offer his condolences. "The death of Lorenzo is an enormous loss for the whole of Florence, just as much as it was when your father passed away. And I feel like I have lost a part of me."

"Thank you, Poggio. In all these years we have known each other, you have always been a man I feel proud to call a friend."

"How are Ginevra and Pierfrancesco taking it?" asked Bracciolini, referring to Lorenzo's wife and son.

"Ginevra is a strong woman, just like all the women of our family," replied Cosimo. "But Pierfrancesco worries me deeply. He is only ten years old, and for a boy his age to lose his father . . ."

Cosimo stopped. His sadness made it difficult to continue.

"Your brother has always been one step behind you," said Bracciolini. "Just like you, he returned from exile and collected antique books and works of art—but not in the same number. And just like you, he covered public offices, but of lesser importance. He even shared your same illness, and many times you attempted to lessen its symptoms together at the thermal baths."

"What is your point?" asked Cosimo.

"That your brother, in his infinite love for you, spent his entire life as your shadow," replied Bracciolini.

"Are you implying my brother did not live a happy existence?" asked Cosimo.

"No, quite the opposite. Since you were little boys you supported each other. I don't think that Lorenzo died with any regret, and you certainly should not have any either." Cosimo was comforted by Bracciolini's words, managing to finally find the strength to ask his reason for wanting to meet him.

"I wish you would deliver the eulogy at my brother's funeral, Poggio. Just like Niccolò da Uzzano delivered the eulogy for my father. I would not want any other person to do it, especially after the words you have just spoken."

Bracciolini put a hand on Cosimo's shoulder, staring into his eyes. "I will do it, Cosimo. I will do it for you."

Beyond this bereavement, Cosimo's reputation took a hard

blow when, in 1441, terrible news ran through the city. The new *gonfaloniere*, Bartolomeo Orlandini, had murdered an old friend of his, Captain Baldaccio di Anghiari, after luring him into a trap in the Signoria's palace, where he attacked him, threw him out of a window, and finally beheaded him.

Baldaccio's small son died tragically shortly after his father's assassination and this further tragedy eventually pushed his young wife, whom Cosimo knew, to transform their home into a convent and retire there in seclusion along with other women.

The motivation behind the murder wasn't clear, but the rumors, which were possibly spread by Cosimo's political adversaries, said that the latter had turned a blind eye, if not outright encouraging the crime, because Neri Capponi was a close friend of Baldaccio. With one word, the captain could have used his troops to overturn Cosimo and hand Florence over into the hands of Capponi.

Perhaps the simplest explanation for the crime could be found in the animosity that had developed between the two men when the victim had harshly criticized the murderer for the cowardice he had demonstrated in battle, during the recently concluded war against Milan.

Pope Eugene was so outraged by that crime that it became for him the signal to finally leave Florence. Cosimo, who was already worn out from being implicated in the murder, tried to convince his old friend, the pontiff not to leave.

"You must know that I had nothing to do with that, Your Holiness," Cosimo swore to him.

"The whole city is moved by the fate of the wife and child of the murdered man, yet you seem more willing to talk about your innocence than what will happen to them," replied the pope.

"You know very well that I would never put myself first unless it was absolutely necessary. You also know that whatever may befall them, Florence will provide to their needs. Lastly, it is my right and duty to defend myself from the poisonous accusations thrown against me," continued Cosimo.

"Then I guess you are not aware of the two poems against me that are circulating in Florence. Both call me crazy because I want to leave the city and your protection to go to Alfonso, King of Naples."

That would be a new letdown for Florence, which was subsidizing the military campaign of Francesco Sforza against Alfonso in order to favor his rival, Renato d'Angiò.

"What are you going to do now, Cosimo? Will you make me a prisoner here in Florence?" said the pope, whose demeanor was so mild-mannered during personal meetings with Cosimo that he rarely appeared to be so decisive and aggressive.

In the grip of frustration, and perhaps remembering the conflict with Pope Martin from a few years before, Cosimo clenched his fists in anger, but for a brief moment. Even though he felt betrayed and humiliated by the accusations that had brought him to this point, Cosimo could impose nothing onto that individual with whom he had had a privileged friendship for many years.

A dejected Cosimo returned to the *palazzo*. On the way, he met Neri Capponi, with whom he was trying to maintain a good relationship after the murder of Baldaccio. With all the negative events that had begun with Lorenzo's death, any crisis caused by disagreement between the two old allies would make matters even worse.

Now Neri stopped Cosimo, as if to show that between the

two of them there was to be no bad blood. Perhaps he was still suspicious about his ally, but Neri knew as much as Cosimo that Florence could not afford a crisis and, on top of that, they both sustained a defeat they could lament together.

"I have been told about the pope," said Neri.

"I sent Giannozzo Manetti to try to talk some sense into him, but it was useless," replied Cosimo, referring to one of the most esteemed Florentine humanists and politicians.

"Do you think that . . . we should try to hold the pope against his will?" asked Neri cautiously.

"And what would it do to us besides creating new enemies?" replied Cosimo.

"And to think that there are people saying that I am the smartest one between us," concluded Neri, lowering his gaze with a long, sad sigh.

To let the pope see that he held no grudges, Cosimo went to witness the departure of Eugene and of his retinue from Santa Maria Novella; Cosimo had also gone there for a more pleasant goal, to greet Poggio Bracciolini, who was obviously about to follow the pope.

"So, you are leaving Florence once again," said Cosimo to his old friend, one of the few who had remained loyal.

"I am sorry. Just when we could have started to discuss Plato," replied Bracciolini.

"You will always be welcome in our 'new Athens,'" replied Cosimo with a hint of a smile.

"You know, I want to tell you that my sources have currently located a copy of . . ." said Bracciolini, trying to cheer up his friend.

"No, do not tell me," interrupted Cosimo. "We shall talk

about our beloved books and your research when you come back to Florence on a more propitious occasion. When, I hope, I shall be able to talk to you about a few new projects I would like to involve you in. Right now, I can only thank you for Lorenzo's eulogy."

Cosimo signaled the pope, who reciprocated sternly.

"Farewell or goodbye, Your Holiness."

"Farewell or goodbye, Cosimo. I still thank you for what you have done." The retinue took its leave from Cosimo, who for the first time in his life felt completely alone.

Cosimo went back to work at the bank and to de facto ruling Florence, trying to find again the motivation that he felt was missing now that he no longer had his brother's support.

"Do you want to talk about him?" Contessina asked one evening. Cosimo did not reply, looking deeply into her eyes until they became watery from tears.

Even for this extremely cold, smart, and calculating man, the disappearance of the dearest person in his life was almost unbearable. Moreover, with that death, Cosimo was forced to face his loss in order to bring changes to the bank.

"I will leave the contract as we originally stipulated it," he said one day to his general managers.

"Would that be legal? Could that cause bureaucratic problems?" asked Salutati, showing little tact.

"No, it won't. Though my brother has passed, I want to feel him close to me for a while longer."

In 1443 Antonio Salutati passed away, which meant that Giovanni Benci became the main manager of the bank. Thanks to the relationship established with Cosimo, who tolerated Benci's peculiar personality, and to the managerial and financial abilities of the latter, the bank went through a period of maximum prosperity.

That period was somewhat useful for Cosimo—it diverted his attention from Lorenzo's death and from those last events that had stained his reputation.

"How is it going with the opening of the Pisan branch, Benci?" asked Cosimo.

"Splendidly. I must admit that our business there has never been better since your cousin Averardo's son died and they had to close their bank there." Benci realized that he had said too much, as he often did.

"With all due respect," he added with belated consideration. Cosimo by now knew Benci and his idiosyncrasies and didn't even take notice of that sentence.

"Try to have some detailed reports as soon as possible," replied Cosimo. "I would like to see how our Italian branches are doing in order to plan the opening of some new ones around Europe."

"Any particular cities in mind?" asked Benci.

"I am thinking of England, most certainly." Benci marked those instructions on a secret book that he filled daily. Even during his worst periods, Cosimo always looked for new solutions to increase or improve business, and kept blindly believing that the directives of all branches must be the same, just like the fact that all decisions had to go through Florence first, especially when he was the one to make them final.

A precursor of his time, he saw the potential to shape business in a tightly connected vertical form.

"The secret, Benci, is to link everything together. My father taught me that many years ago and I have been repeating the same to people like you." Benci listened with pleasure. Even though, as Cosimo often said, he was a more than capable manager, there was always something to learn from a man of his importance.

"If a European branch acquires unprocessed wool and thins it down, then it will send the semi-ready product to Florence in order to have it completed and then re-export it as a finished cloth. Finally, the cloth will be sold on the European markets, maybe even by the very same branch that acquired it first."

In spite of knowing by heart that labor model, out of respect for Cosimo, Benci also marked those last indications on the secret book. "I must thank you, Cosimo. I have been working for the bank since your father's time, but I never thought I could become so rich and pleased about the success of my work," said Benci.

Cosimo replied with his usual irony, a sign that at least he was trying to get over the loss of Lorenzo. "I really hope you did not start working hard only when I raised the profits in your partnership."

The Medici's wealth did not only come out of the bank's profits, but their other ventures had also started to prosper once again: the wool trade had picked up almost to the same level of the old splendor, and Cosimo had a very big influence on that market, because over the years the Medici had become almost the exclusive importers of alum, a necessary product for the dyeing of wool.

The year 1444 arrived, and Cosimo found himself facing another attack on his reputation, caused by a small surge of discontent.

Some matchmakers in his service had put names of relatives of exiled citizens or simply those opposed to Cosimo into the ballot boxes.

The situation found a resolution with the replacement of the matchmakers, and the reasons behind this sabotage are to this day unknown. It seemed to be linked to the increase of the taxes for some social categories. With the substitution of the matchmakers, Cosimo found himself surrounded by loyal men tied to the Medici party through personal interest. Despite the risk this incurred, Cosimo didn't change his attitude, continuing to behave like an almost common citizen and trying to spend as much time as possible in the company of men of letters and artists.

The year 1444 also celebrated the marriage of Piero to Lucrezia Tornabuoni, and Cosimo managed to see the completion of two projects about which he cared very much. The first was the family palace built on land bought in Via Larga before the exile and which had been designed by the faithful Michelozzo. The first architect chosen by the *palazzo* had been Brunelleschi, with whom Cosimo had a heated discussion.

"I know Florentines. Sooner or later, in the future even we Medici will be banished from Florence, but I want to leave something no one could banish—buildings and works of art," Cosimo told Brunelleschi.

When Cosimo first proposed the project, Brunelleschi was dealing with another assignment given to him by the Medici—the re-modernization of the ancient church of San Lorenzo.

"I have finally been asked to make a civil building, and the person asking is someone I admire and who has the means to fulfill my vision. I thank fate and fortune for this opportunity," said the artist proudly. But everything fell through when Cosimo got scared because of the imposing nature of the project delivered to him by Brunelleschi.

"You know how much power envy has on the souls of men. Not just enemies but also friends can be ready to turn against those who might have too much good fortune," said Cosimo.

"Is it because the building would cost too much?" asked an angered Brunelleschi.

"No, it is a matter of evading envy," readily replied Cosimo.

Even though the collaboration between the patron and the artist didn't end, on that occasion Brunelleschi shredded the drawing into a thousand pieces out of rage and returned to his workshop, forcing Cosimo to replace him with Michelozzo.

The second project realized during that year was one that Cosimo cherished even more. It was a plan involving what is considered to be the first public library in Europe, built by Michelozzo in Saint Mark after the "splendid atonement" imposed by Pope Eugene. In a long hall decorated with arches and columns, Cosimo made available to anyone hundreds of books, some from his private collection, others inherited by deceased intellectual friends, such as the great humanist Niccolò Niccoli; others yet purposefully copied by the best scribes in Florence.

For a period of time, Cosimo entrusted his firstborn with the management of the library, which Piero continued to expand with new acquisitions of rare books and with the scrupulous inventory of the ones already possessed. If at times it happened that Cosimo was surprised at his son's abilities in the field of literature, more often it was Piero who was surprised at his father's love for his books, not to mention his astonishing memory.

"May I ask you something, Father?" asked Piero one day.

"Is it something about books?" replied Cosimo.

"Yes, it is something about books. I was wondering why you almost never reread some of them," asked Piero.

"Oh, it is quite simple," replied Cosimo. "I was born with, or perhaps I have developed over the years, the capacity to read any book and remember all its details for years and years. And I am not just referring to its contents."

Piero took an old German volume from the pile of the recent books brought to the library, dusty and forgotten among the many volumes of greater value, perhaps acquired by Cosimo decades before during the journey to Constance, and never opened since. The young man opened the book, read a small detail in the first page, and looked at his father with an air of defiance.

"Then I believe you would surely remember, Father, the peculiarity that this volume holds," said Piero.

Cosimo bent his head slightly in order to look at the bound cover and spine of the volume, then without any hesitation gave the correct answer. "Is it the one with the signature that reads 'Kruger A., accountant'?"

Piero reopened the book, quietly looking at that signature several times, incapable of understanding how his father could have remembered that detail after so many decades.

As it had already happened in 1435 and in 1439, in 1445 Cosimo occupied for the third and last time the post of Gonfaloniere di Giustizia after a regular draw, but only a few years after a major event put back in motion plans that he had devised some time before.

In 1447 the Duke of Milan died, and almost immediately, with the help of Medici financing, Sforza claimed power by proclaiming himself lord of Milan. With that peculiar alliance arranged years before with the *condottiero*, Cosimo had been in the right once more, and Florence found itself allied with the ancient Milanese enemies.

"You will go to Milan to bring our congratulations to Sforza," Cosimo announced to Piero and Neri Capponi.

"You should come with us, Cosimo. The idea of bringing Sforza to Florence was yours and yours only," replied Neri.

"Sforza asked me to open a branch of the bank there and gift to me a house. I will go see him, but I am just too tired right now," replied Cosimo faintly, feeling the weight of the years, of ill health, and of too many commitments.

Even though he was tired in his body, Cosimo's intuitions continued to be accurate in the same way that good fortune so often had accompanied him in life. In addition to accepting Sforza's power grab, Cosimo made peace again for a time with Alfonso, who had deposed his rival from the throne of Naples, sending him as a token of peace an ancient Latin volume.

When Pope Eugene died, Cosimo found himself immediately in the good graces of the new pontiff, Nicholas V, a humanist who had a special place in his heart for patrons and men of letters.

But Cosimo missed Lorenzo terribly, and for this he always considered his brother's family as his own, leaving his fortune undivided until Pierfrancesco would reach maturity. When this happened in 1451, half of the family's wealth, also comprising the two Mugellan villas of Cafaggiolo and Trebbio, was allocated to the young man.

In spite of Cosimo asking him to stay in the palace of Via Larga, Pierfrancesco lived mainly at Mugello, preferring hunting and entertainment to art and literature. On the rare occasions when uncle and nephew met, Cosimo tried to instill some of his own spirit into the young man. Most of the time those attempts were unfruitful, and Cosimo struggled to recognize his brother's spirit in this nephew, whose intellect was not a very curious one.

"Your father also cared about taking care of his intellect by feeding it with the sacred fire of culture," said Cosimo.

"I am different from you and my father, Uncle," answered Pierfrancesco with disarming sincerity. "The joys you feel when you are surrounded by your Greek or Latin codices, or your philosophy treatises, come for me by spending time hunting with my horses and my dogs."

"I know that well, just as I know how different you are from my firstborn Piero. But you understand family must remain united," replied Cosimo. Pierfrancesco disciplined himself to just stare at his uncle and nod, but it was with him that the two branches of the Medici family began to diverge.

When Piero died, the relationship between Lorenzo the Magnificent and Pierfrancesco became cold and distant, and until the city's fate rested in the hands of Lorenzo, Pierfrancesco's sons (whom Lorenzo the Magnificent had adopted at their father's death) had to remain in the background of power.

Those years continued to be turbulent: Venice was furious with the old Florentine allies and Naples was trying to invade Milan, which had been weakened by a change of regime.

"That is bad news. We are forced to close the branches in Venice and Naples. The Florentines living here are being sent into exile," a worried Benci said to Cosimo.

"But how is the new branch in Milan going?" asked Cosimo.

"It could not be any better. Sforza cannot do without us, even if some people claim it is because he owes you a huge sum of money and . . ."

"I know what you are about to say, Benci. That we should be worried about Naples and Venice," Cosimo anticipated, his tired and marked face showing the signs of a night spent suffering in the throes of arthritic pains. "But we should let matters run their course. They may settle or not and we should adapt to them. You see, I know that you cannot run a state on prayers, but I am also certain of one other thing: Apart from religion, commerce is what unifies men. Wars may pass, but the need to trade with others will always remain."

Benci made a little gesture of assent. It wasn't that he didn't believe Cosimo's words, but he was unused to seeing him so tired and lifeless.

"Believe me, solutions will find their way, one way or another," concluded Cosimo.

The Emperor of the Sacred Roman Empire demanded the cessation of the alliance between Florence and Milan, and Cosimo was forced to ask the King of France for support, risking new major problems for the whole of Italy, given the ambitions of invasion that France had expressed.

Furious because of Florence's moves, King Alfonso sent an army guided by his son from Naples to invade the city, unleashing for the first time and in a concrete manner the rage of Florentine people against Cosimo. They gathered under the palace of the Signoria and under the very home of the Medici in Via Larga in order to protest.

The people of Florence, who had borne for decades the increase in taxes to sustain the costs of the war, and who in a normal situation would not have thought to revolt against Cosimo, had reached a point of exasperation. The council's safe boxes were practically empty, the danger of an invasion from King Alfonso or the betrayal from the French were both more than possible scenarios, and all this was aggravated by the immobility of the mercenary troops hired to defend Florence.

It would be his usual luck and coincidence that saved Cosimo. The political situation calmed down fairly quickly when the French army intervened against the attempted invasion of Florence, and with the Turkish reconquest of Constantinople, putting an end to all of the other Italian conflicts by creating a state of emergency on the peninsula.

Many of the religious people and men of letters that Cosimo had met during the Florentine Council died during the Turkish invasion, but some managed to save themselves; having predicted the disaster, they moved outside of Constantinople, many to Italy.

United against a common enemy, the main Italian cities signed a peace treaty in Lodi in 1454 to then unite in a holy anti-Turkish league a few months after. Those decades of peace established at Lodi would help even more the development of the art and culture of the Renaissance.

Florence was financially exhausted for the costs sustained during the last wars, and Cosimo was accused of being a war-monger blinded by his expansionist goals. The consensus in regard to the Medici patriarch wasn't unanimous, and some political adversaries or poorly loyal allies were already scheming to stab him in the back.

Cosimo now accepted his own decline and understood that he was no longer the man he once used to be, increasingly retiring behind the scenes. Piero took his father's place in political matters, while Giovanni assumed management of the bank, with unfortunate outcomes at the death of Giovanni Benci in 1455.

Cosimo wasn't entirely removed from the power games, because at the death of Neri Capponi in 1457 he tried to carry out a constitutional reform with the help of his supporter Luca

Pitti, an ambiguous man who looked after the concentration of his personal power more often than Florence's interest, to the point of scheming against Piero after Cosimo's death. Furthermore, in 1459, with help from Giovanni, who was unparalleled in this kind of matter, he organized two big parties for Francesco Sforza's adolescent son and the new Pope Pius II's visit to Florence.

"Why don't you eat or drink something, Father?" Giovanni asked Cosimo, while inebriated in the amusement of the party but still attentive enough to make sure that all guests be served as they should.

Cosimo, who attended the event as his duty, shook his head, replying desolately. "I am only here because I have to, my son. I cannot eat nor drink any more what is served during this sort of celebration."

But Giovanni had also the merit of introducing to his father someone who could cheer up the man's twilight years in 1458. This person was the young Marsilio Ficino, son of Cosimo's personal doctor. That brilliant young man, so inclined toward philosophy, was ideal for Cosimo's project of making Florence the new Athens.

The aged patron and his protegé often walked along the Careggi villa to talk about philosophy and moral questions.

"My tutor de' Rossi never properly taught me Plato's philosophy, but rather all of Aristotle's works. I envy you," said Cosimo.

"But I did not have the chance to meet Pletone and Bessarione in person like you did during the council in Florence. So we must say that our envy is mutual," replied Ficino.

"Do you feel envious for my being so much older than you?" asked Cosimo with a note of humor in his voice.

"Well, I think getting old is a matter that . . ."

Little Lorenzo ran to his grandfather, pushing aside the guest and holding in his hand a branch that had fallen from a tree of the estate and a small blade.

"Please, Grandfather, carve me a little flute from this tree branch!" begged the child. Cosimo tried to please his grandson, but his wrinkled hand, plagued by arthritis, could not maneuver the blade. With a delicate gesture, without humiliating his host, Ficino took the branch and the blade in his hands and started to carve out the flute.

"Here, Cosimo, let me do that. These tasks aren't worthy of the ruler of Florence."

"Careful," said Cosimo, saving himself from the embarrassment of the situation with a joke. "If you keep going along with his requests, he might even ask you to play that flute you're carving."

"Thank you, Signore! Thank you, Grandfather!" exclaimed Lorenzo, running away with that newly created instrument.

"You see, Cosimo," said Ficino, "the matter that composed that flute was the branch of an oak, but even an oak is nothing without being wood first. Just like a statue is nothing without marble and marble is nothing without a rock."

"What does that mean?" asked Cosimo.

"If we take any meaning out of matter, only indefinite chaos will remain. And therefore, just like Plato, I think it is more rewarding to work on incorporeal things, because matter is nothing without a shape."

Cosimo nodded, fascinated by the young man's wisdom.

"You talk about chaos and emptiness. Can you perhaps tell me if there is something after death?" asked Cosimo.

"I will tell you if I get there before you!" exclaimed Ficino.

"I knew I chose you well!" said Cosimo, amused by Ficino's joke, which bore the mark of a morbid sense of humor very much like his own.

"It is amusing," continued Cosimo. "I, by the name Medici, I am seeking your collaboration, the son of a medic, asking you to become a doctor of souls through philosophy. I want you to be at the head of the Platonic Academy that I wish to establish. The academy will bring Florence even closer to Athens, and you shall read Plato to all the most important intellectuals in and outside of Florence, such as my dear friend Poggio Bracciolini. And you will be with me to talk about philosophy."

"I am flattered," said Ficino modestly. "But I cannot abuse your hospitality and I do not have the means to buy a house near yours . . ."

Cosimo pointed to a small villa that was being built next to his. "You see that house? I am having it restructured for you. You will live there and, if you want, you could also use it for the academy."

Far away from Florentine politics, from wars and the pressure of the bank and commerce, Cosimo tried to spend more time with his family. In 1459, by now a patron of the arts for his whole life, he found himself part of a work of art. Almost twenty years had gone by since the council in Florence, and Cosimo now decided to have a painting done to remember that event in his palace on Via Larga, inside the family chapel.

He had been painted and sculpted before, but now he was more old and frail and hence not very inclined to model. Yet Cosimo wanted to remember in a special way that event which had brought him so close to Platonic philosophy.

"You have studied under Beato Angelico, am I right?" asked Cosimo to Benozzo di Lese, the artist chosen to paint the fresco.

Benozzo was a painter known for a style rich in details and had been originally called by Cosimo to paint a different kind of fresco altogether.

"I was told you want me to paint a portrait of your grand-children, signor Cosimo," said Benozzo.

"I have changed my mind," replied Cosimo with a feeble voice.

"Oh, I am sorry to hear that. Perhaps you did not like the paintings I have shown you? You want to give this work to another artist?" asked Benozzo.

"No, rather the opposite. I have the utmost faith in you, and your work is going to be much bigger." Cosimo slowly opened his hand and pointed at the members of the family present for that meeting: Contessina, his sons, and all of his grandchildren.

"You will paint us all. I will tell you how to portray some people who cannot be with us. And you will paint us during a specific event."

Benozzo surpassed himself, completing the work in a few months with the help of only a few assistants and the probable supervision of Piero. The fresco represented the procession of the Magi, referring at the same time to the Florentine Council and the grandeur of the Medici through the main members of the family and their dearest friends. Practically everyone was there, including Ficino and the same Benozzo.

After it was finished, Cosimo lightly touched the fresco, lingering on the image of the grandchildren. Those figures made so perfect and idealized appeased him, and made him think with tenderness about the future, even about the one he himself would not see.

But every time his gaze fell on his own image, Cosimo was tormented about the last years and the life he had lived. He worried about whether the Medici would remain in Florence or be sent into exile, whether his palaces would still be standing, how many would remember him? How many would recognize what he had done for Florence and for his family?

Seeing her husband in such a state, Contessina hugged him by his shoulders, gently kissing the back of his head. "With your guidance, Florence will thrive for a thousand more years, Cosimo," she murmured in his ear.

"Cosimo, Cosimo, Cosimo." The man lifted his gaze, hearing his wife calling him dozens, hundreds, thousands of times. Cosimo met Contessina's eyes—she was trying to wake him up. In a few moments, after having relived all of his life, Cosimo's memories dissolved as he came back into the present.

"You closed your eyes for a moment. I was getting worried," said Contessina.

"No, you must not. I just needed a moment to rest. Yes, to rest," replied Cosimo.

The year before, immediately after Benozzo completed the Magi Chapel, Giovanni lost his son Cosimino, ending in tragedy a year that had seemed to be one of tranquility. That misfortune would not even be the last of the losses that Cosimo would experience.

Tired and tormented by his thoughts, Cosimo went to visit Ficino in the small villa that he had built for him. The day was ending and the sun was leaving, replaced by an evening breeze. The philosopher opened the door, finding the old patriarch pale as a sheet before him. "Sit down, my friend. You do not look too well," said Ficino.

"My house is too big for such a small family and that is why I decided to bother you in yours," replied Cosimo.

"Don't say that," said Ficino. "You have plenty of relatives and friends who love you and who are happy to have you with them."

Cosimo pointed at a philosophy book that Ficino kept on the entrance table. "Another day closes," he said. "And I am here because I would like to know from you what happiness is and how to find it."

Ficino took a book in his hand, opened it, and began reading a passage. "What is happiness? Perhaps, as we get older, life becomes a burden and death becomes a reward?"

"It is true, it is all true . . ." Cosimo replied feebly while closing his eyes.

"Why are you closing your eyes? Are you not well?" asked Ficino.

"I am trying to get them used to eternal sleep!" replied Cosimo with a sudden burst of humor. Patron and pupil started to laugh as if they were two mindless young men.

"Will you read Plato when my time comes? Will you bring a *cithara* to my funeral?" added Cosimo.

"I promise you, I will. And you will have a simple funeral, without frills, as befits every great man of letters."

"That is just what I want. Thank you. Now I know I can leave this world in peace. And you are right, I have a good family and good friends. Perhaps, good enemies."

Epilogue

osimo didn't die in 1460, but rather on August 1, 1464, at
ten in the evening, at the age of seventy-five.

He died peacefully, in his own bed, after having risen to
attend mass for the last time in the family chapel.

Piero scrupulously marked down the account notes relative
to the expenses for the funeral, including details of the mourning
clothes for the family and servants. Even though he had never
become entirely accustomed to the work at the bank, Piero was
still a Medici, after all.

Contrary to the deceased's request, the Signoria organized
a solemn funeral service to pay him the highest honors. Common people, intellectuals, politicians, and representatives of all
Italian and foreign states attended the funeral in San Lorenzo.
And together with them, there were all the workers of the bank,
from the managers to the employees all the way down to the
messengers.

After the function, Cosimo's body was laid down in a coffin

in the underground crypt, and the honorific title of *Pater Patriae*, father of the country, was engraved on his tombstone. Standing in front of Cosimo's coffin along with Contessina, Piero read the engraving over and over, thinking of all the definitions given to his father during his life: "brilliant businessman," "astute politician," "enlightened intellectual."

"Yet he always remained a modest, reserved man," Piero told Contessina, "full of human flaws."

"Those flaws are what made us love him so much," replied Contessina. "It never mattered how much he achieved, he was still our Cosimo."

The dim light of the candles kept shining on that beautifully built coffin.

"He always said he wanted to be remembered at least for the buildings he had built," added Contessina. "I wonder how much he knew . . ."

". . . That he left us the biggest legacy one could ever possibly imagine," concluded Piero while looking at Lorenzo entering the crypt to pay his final tribute to his grandfather.

"Say goodbye to your grandfather, Lorenzo. Then we shall return home," Piero told him.

"What will we do, Father?"

"You will see, son. You will see."

Cosimo had died, but his greatness had not. The future of Florence had already been written, and it was a bright one, just like that day of summer when a grandfather was telling stories to his favorite grandchild.

About the Author

Francesco Massaccesi (Pescara, 1985) is an Italian screenwriter. A committed scholar of world cinema, he has authored and collaborated on several Italian and international magazines and books, as well as having worked in different fields of the film industry. An avid reader and researcher, his interest in history spans from antiquity to contemporaneity.

NOW AVAILABLE FROM THE MENTORIS PROJECT

America's Forgotten Founding Father
A Novel Based on the Life of Filippo Mazzei
by Rosanne Welch

A. P. Giannini—The People's Banker
by Francesca Valente

Building Heaven's Ceiling
A Novel Based on the Life of Filippo Brunelleschi
by Joe Cline

Christopher Columbus: His Life and Discoveries
by Mario Di Giovanni

Dreams of Discovery
A Novel Based on the Life of the Explorer John Cabot
by Jule Selbo

The Faithful
A Novel Based on the Life of Giuseppe Verdi
by Collin Mitchell

Fermi's Gifts
A Novel Based on the Life of Enrico Fermi
by Kate Fuglei

Saving the Republic
A Novel Based on the Life of Marcus Cicero
by Eric D. Martin

Soldier, Diplomat, Archaeologist
A Novel Based on the Bold Life of Louis Palma di Cesnola
by Peg A. Lamphier

The Soul of a Child
A Novel Based on the Life of Maria Montessori
by Kate Fuglei

FUTURE TITLES FROM THE MENTORIS PROJECT

A Biography about Alessandro Volta
Cycles of Wealth
Fulfilling the Promise of California
A Novel Based on the Life of Amerigo Vespucci
A Novel Based on the Life of Andrea Doria
A Novel Based on the Life of Andrea Palladio
A Novel Based on the Life of Angela Bambace
A Novel Based on the Life of Angelo Dundee
A Novel Based on the Life of Antonin Scalia
A Novel Based on the Life of Antonio Meucci
A Novel Based on the Life of Artemisia Gentileschi
A Novel Based on the Life of Buzzie Bavasi
A Novel Based on the Life of Cesare Becaria
A Novel Based on the Life of Father Matteo Ricci
A Novel Based on the Life of Federico Fellini
A Novel Based on the Life of Frank Capra

For more information on these titles and
The Mentoris Project, please visit
www.mentorisproject.org.

Made in the USA
Monee, IL
01 May 2020

29061696R00146